THE ACCORD

THE ACCORD

TOWARDS UNIVERSAL ONENESS

Adam Reddy

PARTRIDGE

A Penguin Random House Company

To order additional copies of this book, contact
Partridge India
000 800 10062 62
orders.india@partridgepublishing.com

www.partridgepublishing.com/india

Acknowledgements

I would like to express my gratitude to my sister Sirisha and my spouse, Mahi, who saw me through this book, and all those who have supported me in writing this book.

Chapter 1

21 April 2021, Miami

The first-of-its-kind meeting had begun. Ten most intelligent people from ten most influential countries were invited. Mr Jonathan Reynolds, chief secretary of the organization One World, One People, started his speech.

'One World, One People—although it sounds impossible, there is no such thing as impossible with the outstanding resolve of human beings. That's what I believe, and that's what history says. The famous saying "Religion is for people, and people are not for religion" would be a reality soon. Over the years, we have proudly seen our inventions and success in terms of technology and science. It is not very far, ladies and gentlemen, and we will shortly see our colonies in various other planets in the universe. I feel proud of the progress we have made in the field of science and technology, but on the other hand, I feel sorry for millions of my brothers and sisters living under barriers called culture and religion. Why was religion made? Can anyone answer my question, my dear friends?'

'I am Dr Sarah Jackson, doctor from the USA. Well, I guess religion was made to show the right path for better living and to define the roles and responsibilities of human beings.'

'That's great, Sarah, well answered. One big round of applause for Sarah,' said Jonathan.

Claps followed, which rejuvenated the mood in the meeting room.

'Yes, religion is there to show us the way forward in our lives. However, it has been dragging us back. I really feel ashamed of religious fundamentalism and strikes on religious lines, strikes based on race, creed, and colour. In this era of rocket science, we still come across people who kill fellow humans on the pretext of honour. Time and again, religion has failed to curb crime, corruption, racism, and starvation. Poor people are becoming poorer, and the rich are getting richer. Now I ask each one of you in this room, why did all contemporary religions fail to deliver the permanent solution for the ongoing tussle between religions and groups? I am not directing to any single religion or sect, but I blame everyone in this regard.

'Now I ask each of you all whether this is not like dragging us back. Today, we have excellent scientists, fantastic engineers, and outstanding biologists. But I am afraid they have failed miserably to concentrate on social issues. They sacrifice their entire lives to create something but, at the same time, forget about what exactly gives solace to humans.

'Please tell me if you need any clarification. I don't want to take much precious time of yours, and I always prefer to take short and crispy speeches. This meeting seems to have taken much longer time than I expected. It has been two hours, and people seem to be very attentive. Thanks for your focus on the subject. Well, the sole aim of this meeting is to take your valuable suggestions on our new concept One World, One People.

'There are various stumbling blocks, but they can be made into constructive steps. Remember, Rome was not built in a day. We will arrange more such meetings every year, with more number of participants.'

'Mr Jonathan Reynolds, I really appreciate such meeting, and I believe that religion should take us forward. But religion has been surely taking us to Stone Age once again. You are pitching for one religion for one world. I would rather advocate no religion for this world. What is your take on it?'

'Your name, profession, and country, please? This will help me to understand you better.'

'I am Anirudh Vedanta from India, scientist by profession.'

'Thank you, Mr Anirudh, for your good question. Perhaps you have gone the extra mile. Ha ha ha! I really appreciate your thought. I would rather expect the answer from you yourself, Mr Anirudh. For instance, let us imagine that law has been relaxed for one day in your country India, then what will happen?'

'There is a possibility that there would be a large number of cases of rapes, murders, and lootings all across the country,' replied Anirudh.

'Good. I was expecting that answer from you, Mr Anirudh. And yes, I do agree with you as people's mindsets are different and they tend to react differently at various situations. So have you ever imagined what will happen to people when they are made to believe that there is no God at all? The world will go down before its time. Scientists, doctors, lawyers, or professors may be civilized enough to think correctly and take the right decisions with their intelligence. However, there are more people who are just followers and let others make decisions on their behalf, and they can't even digest if they realize that there is no one there to help them. So the world becoming irreligious is not going to be a reality for a long time to come. I hope that explanation answers your question, gentlemen,' said Mr Reynolds.

'Yes, I got my answer. Thank you,' replied Anirudh.

'You all might be wondering why you people were called for this meeting, and some people are viewing it as another conspiracy by the USA to control world politics in the name of One World, One People But there is no truth to these concerns. As I have already told you all before starting my speech, we are a voluntary organization and are certainly not American secret agency people. We have only made a study with statistics on economies related to the ill effects of excessive fundamentalism based on religion. After conducting the study on this issue, we have also forecast the challenges that mankind is going to face if the problem is not solved. If you have questions, please feel free to ask me.'

'As-salaam alaikum, I am Sheikh Ibrahim, professor in religious studies from Ethiopia. I have a question to Mr Jonathan. I am viewing this as a clear propaganda of

Christianity to take over the rest of the religions across the world. It is a well-known fact that one religion does not guarantee oneness as it has been evident in many instances. The ongoing insurgency between sects within one religion around the world says it all.'

'Great Point, Ibrahim. You know there are a few questions which give a scope to open up personally.' Mr Reynolds laughed. 'Well, personally, I don't consider myself a complete Christian as my father is a Christian, my mother is a Jew, and my wife is a Muslim from Lebanon. Now, can I be called a Christian just because I have a Christian name? Our society One World, One people has been formed by twenty different people who belong to different religions and races and don't have any connection to any Christian missionary.

'Your second question is a more serious one. Well, I believe there has been human interference in dividing one religion into different sects, and the same is applicable to almost all religions. In our endeavour, we are not asking you to ditch your existing religion, but we are trying to create such a medium where all religions come together by sharing tenets from all religions and where tolerance and acceptance are the foundation. I would rather call it a universal brotherhood rather than a new religion. Any more questions, please?'

'Yes, Mr Reynolds. I am Sukvinder Singh, a social scientist from Canada. My question is whether religion works without God. For believers, it is the power of God which runs the religion. The belief in God serves as a motivation for a normal person to pray when in sorrow or in happiness.

Are you trying to create a new religion without a creator? Please answer, Mr Reynolds.'

'Well, every religion is governed by unique rules and regulations, and God is common amongst all religions. This has been accepted by people of all religions, mostly. There is no second thought on this issue. Therefore, if one common god can serve all existing religions, why can't that very same god be applied to my new concept of oneness or new religion?' replied Jonathan. 'Ladies and gentlemen, this concludes today's meeting on One World, One People. Kindly be in touch with your valuable suggestions through www.oneworld-onepeople.com.

'Now I require a few volunteers for my journey. You all have already proved your mettle in your chosen fields, and we need people like you to make things happen more effectively. I know not all deeds are all about the money. Therefore, I have placed you an offer to work with us for a noble cause. You may contact me with your valid questions and expectations any time.

'Okay! I really thank you all for attending this meeting and making it a success. You can be part of our society and pave the way for the new world. Furthermore, our intention is to create a better world for tomorrow and not to hurt anyone's sentiments. Good day! I am Jonathan. You may be in touch with me through email or my mobile number.'

Chapter 2

Anirudh was in the elevator, heading back to the hotel room. Sarah and Ibrahim were also present in the same elevator. 'It is like looking for a needle in a haystack, isn't it, guys?' asserted Anirudh.

'Yeah! His offer seems to be like making fish of one and flesh of another,' said Ibrahim.

'I believe it was a good offer to be part of his team to make hay while the sun shines,' replied Sarah.

'Well, he is asking us to volunteer in his dream with clandestine intentions,' said Anirudh.

'Dreams are always clandestine. That's his personal dream, but if the offer fits in with our requirement, we can consider it,' replied Sarah.

'It is not that easy, guys. Some people who are sponsoring this project may have vested interests. The detail given by Jonathan is minimal. There is more to it. Perhaps, it has lots of money angle and more to do with businessmen and industrialists,' said Anirudh.

'Can we meet tonight at the hotel pub at 7 p.m.?' asked Anirudh.

Sarah and Ibrahim nodded in affirmation.

7 p.m., hotel's Finesse Pub

Sarah was first to reach the pub. She has always been punctual in her entire life. This discipline has been instrumental behind her outstanding victories in the field of surgery. Apart from her intellect, she is one of the most good-looking doctors in New York. Patients in New York and most parts of the USA throng for her appointment just to see her mesmerizing smile and healing touch.

'Good evening, guys,' greeted Sarah.

'Good evening, Sarah,' Anirudh and Ibrahim greeted back.

'Thanks, guys, for coming. May I offer you a drink?'

'I will take Coke as I am non-alcoholic,' replied Ibrahim.

'Okay. Gin would be fine for you, Sarah?'

'No, I will go for red wine,' replied Sarah.

Anirudh was smitten by her appealing appearance. She looked splendid in her light-pinkish top and denim trousers. Her medium build with evenly built bust, strawberry-like lips, deep-blue eyes, and long blonde hair touching her shoulders would amaze even the lifeless monument and might arouse the feeble.

'Fine, yeah. Waiter, one Coke, one whisky, large, and one mug of red wine, please. Please get any good dry item as a snack.'

'Fine, sir,' said the waiter.

The Accord

'From where are you in India?' asked Sarah.

'I am from New Delhi basically. I am staying at Bangalore, working for ISRO, Indian Space Research Organization. I am also a visiting professor at the University of Chennai and IIT Hyderabad. Recently, I have successfully tested the first indigenously built *robot* for defence purposes.'

'So you have expertise in making rockets and robots?' asked Sarah.

'Oh yeah! I have spent about six years on them. I have visited Japan twice in this regard. I feel the future is in robotics. Presently, Japan seems to be topping robotics engineering.'

'Righty,' said Anirudh. 'The robots are gonna play an important role in medical services too. There are a number of surgeries successfully dealt by robots across the world,' said Sarah.

'You are a doctor, right? What is your specialization?' asked Anirudh.

'I am a cancer specialist, and I am doing a research in the University of Newark. I have been working very hard on my research, but you know, cancer is such a stubborn disease. It looks as if it may take years to get a breakthrough in cancer research.'

'Oh, you are doing such a noble thing. Certainly appreciable, isn't it, Ibrahim?' asked Anirudh.

'Yes, she deserves it,' said Ibrahim.

'Ibrahim is eager to hear from you. All the while, we have been doing the talking work without any luck of hearing from him,' said Anirudh, and they laughed.

'I am a specialist in religious studies, and I have done a research on many great religions in the world. But lately, I have stopped doing anything further as I have taken the responsibility to motivate the children in my country and other fellow African nations. You know, Africa is the worst hit due to civil wars. My dream is to see all children in Africa going to school rather than holding weapons. After all, children are the future and the only hope left for change in Africa. Personally, I have a family in Ethiopia—a wife and four children.'

'That's great, what you are doing for your nation,' said Anirudh.

'Serving the nations gives utmost happiness. That's really an outstanding work. I wish your family best wishes,' said Sarah.

'Good to hear that you have a family, Ibrahim,' said Anirudh.

'You are not married?' asked Ibrahim.

'No, not yet, guys. I have no time to think about my personal life.'

'What about you, Sarah?' asked Ibrahim.

'Never married. I was living with a partner, but now I am single.'

'Oh, that's great too. Living single is wonderful as that is the time to rejuvenate ourselves and start afresh. Sometimes I wish I could be single, but that's never going to happen with family responsibility on my shoulders,' said Ibrahim.

A sudden silence followed. It was fifteen minutes since there was any sort of serious conversation. Sarah was busy working on her tab, Ibrahim was busy watching National Geographic Channel, and Anirudh was having drink after drink.

Anirudh thought, *I will take responsibility of breaking the ice.*

'Hey, guys. Sorry to disturb you people. You seem to be very much occupied,' said Anirudh.

They laughed. 'Not really,' replied Ibrahim.

'Shall we order food?'

'Oh, not at all! Oh sorry, did I surprise you guys? I mean, I was actually thinking of asking something. I will only ask if you are honest to share with me.'

'Yeah, go on,' said Sarah as if watching a suspense thriller.

'Did you get any call from Mr Jonathan and his company today afternoon?'

'What call are you talking about?' replied Sarah.

'Come on, guys, you can trust me as you have trusted those guys,' said Anirudh.

Sarah was tight-lipped and pretending.

'Okay, you tell me, Ibrahim. I know you never lie and not at all permitted.'

'Ahhhhh! Maybe I got a call!' replied Ibrahim.

'Okay, I got an answer from both of you, guys. Now I will share my experience with you. I received a call from Jonathan, and he had offering a huge package for a job offer I have not committed anything to him yet, but I will get back to him in twenty-four hours.'

'Did you ask anything about the project?' asked Sarah.

'Yes, I have asked about the project, and all he has told me was that it is a legitimate project. I guess the project has definitely something to do with today's seminar. But I am totally clueless as to how I fit in to that. I mean, being an atheist, I may not be an adequate person to join the campaign, and moreover, I have spearheaded agitation on blind belief in India. Now I totally fail to understand what my role is going to be.'

Sarah now looked clearly, and she smilingly revealed, 'Yes, I have received a similar type of offer, but only Jesus knows about the project.'

'So, guys, be prepared to receive a call again, and this time, they will call for a meeting with the three of us, if my expectation doesn't go wrong,' said Anirudh.

'What makes you think so?' asked Ibrahim.

'They have sponsored our trip with the sole aim of recruiting us in to their project. Therefore, it's emphatic that they will call us,' replied Anirudh.

'Hey, what is your opinion about Jonathan?' asked Sarah.

'We are being watched from every corner and even now. I think there are big heads involved in this and Jonathan is just like us. Our only difference is that we were called based on the expertise we have achieved in our respective subjects, whereas Jonathan must have been chosen to give excellent speeches. I guess he might be from any sales management team.'

Sarah asked, 'So what do you think, Anirudh, shall we accept the offer? The amount they have offered is whopping.'

'See, guys, it is a very hard decision to make, and I leave it entirely on yourselves. But one thing is for sure—they are very serious about the plan, and somebody else will take the offer if you are not going to take it. My intention is to gamble by taking the offer and really know about their intentions. If I find any kind of irregularity, I will definitely go against them as I don't care for my life and, fortunately, there is no one who cares for my life.'

'Don't ever say that again! Now I am here, and I care about you, Anirudh,' said Sarah.

'Oh, are you hitting on me, dear, thinking that I am single and available? If you think that way, then you are seriously . . . correct,' replied Anirudh, laughing.

Next day, 12.30 p.m., Anirudh received an anonymous call.

'Hello, good afternoon! is it Mr Anirudh speaking?'

'Yeah! This is Anirudh.'

'I am Takashi, personal assistant of Mr Jonathan Reynolds. Mr Reynolds is hosting an important meeting and requests your presence at conference room 4 by 1.30 p.m.'

'Kindly confirm your attendance.'

'Okay, I confirm my attendance.'

'Thank you, sir.'

Chapter 3

Conference room 4, 12.25 p.m.

'You are asking what will happen next. As you make your bed, you must lie on it,' asserted Anirudh.

Meanwhile, Mr Jonathan arrived in the lobby.

Sarah murmured, 'See, he looks like a wolf in sheep's clothing.'

Ibrahim tried to respond but stopped as Mr Jonathan had entered into the conference room.

'Good afternoon, ladies and gentlemen.'

'Welcome aboard to our project. We call it One World, One People.'

'As you know, my name is Jonathan Reynolds. You may call me just Jon.'

'Meet my personal assistant, Mr Takashi. He will be your point of contact from here on, and in any case you need my presence, I am always available for you.'

'Do I make myself clear, ladies and gentlemen?'

'Yes,' said the three of them.

'Jon, I would like to know more about the project. If you could just explain elaborately the necessity and goal of your project, that would be great!'

'Oh, certainly! Why not? You have every right to know it before signing the contract papers. I will put it this way. You people are about to make history! Your names will be written in history, and people will know you for ages to come. You will be given status equivalent to sainthood. All you have to do is make a super being! Every one of us from our childhood has imagined God to be a super being. We have been running on the rules and regulations set by religion or God or a super power. Whatever be the name of the religion doesn't matter to us. We are always governed by rules, rules, and rules and never enjoyed the essence of true life. Have you ever imagined how much we limit ourselves in the process of following these rules?'

'Oh yeah! Only people who believe in religion lose,' said Anirudh.

'I know how hard it is on your part to lose your family in an accident, but do you think that was an accident that took away their lives and made you an orphan?'

Anirudh suddenly turned red and asked, 'Tell me what you know about my parents' death.'

'What I know? I need not work extra hours to enquire about your family and how they died. You have already revealed it in an interview which was telecast. More importantly, they were killed in an accident while they were on their way to a holy place of worship. It really hurts, and I can understand the trauma you had undergone.'

Anirudh became annoyed. 'My belief in religion has nothing to do with my parents' death. I have been an atheist since my childhood days. Death is bound to happen to everyone one day. I know my parents' departure was an irreparable loss, but I always believed in myself and I am a fighter,' said Anirudh.

'Yes, I really appreciate your fighting spirit. The way you have come up in life has been remarkable. Now you are to become a pioneer across the world for paving the way to the creation of an advanced humanoid robot which creates its own power source,' said Jon.

'I suppose we are here to discuss something which changes the Phase of the world completely and certainly not here to highlight my personal achievement,' said Anirudh rather impatiently.

'Yes, I am discussing the same, and I have no intention to intrude in your personal life. People are losing faith in God, and as per survey, we have seen that the belief in God will be reduced to a mere 15 per cent across the globe. We are attempting to cultivate belief in the minds of people by making them understand that God exists. In doing that, we require some outstanding people to do some outstanding things,' said Jon.

'Agreed, but you are not getting to the point on what your plan is or what you want us to do for you. We agreed to your offer, eyeing the package you are offering, but I will make it clear that I will not do anything which is illegal,' said Ibrahim.

'Yes, we agree with what Ibrahim says, and the same applies to us,' said Sarah.

'Once and for all, I will reiterate that you are being chosen to do a legal project, and the company will never insist that you do any work which has not been discussed. I think this clears all your fears on the project, and I request you to bear some time so as to make you understand the job you will be entrusted. I mean, there are some tasks which can't be told in a nutshell,' said Jon. 'During the golden era of religions, the people were so drawn to God that religion was given utmost importance in civilized societies. That was the period when many new religions surfaced. The culture was such that being an atheist was seen as taboo. Now the circumstances have changed drastically. People are so much driven towards science and technology that they have started questioning each and every thing related to God. Criticism of God has been omnipresent in various societies. Questioning the sanctity of anything is good, but cynicism has led people to believe in anti-religious doctrines. The effect is just showing as now there are diminishing family values, disbelief in marriages, and overall increase in crime rate. This is going to be a severe problem by 2050, when humans are likely to divide themselves into various groups based on their DNA samples, and people who are rejected based on DNA test will resort to terrorism and violence, which can be devastating.' Jon paused.

'Yes, you have explained your prophecies, but I don't think it will ever lead to such circumstances as I still come across people who are true believers of God, and I, being religious in every respect, feel optimistic that time will take its course, and we have nothing to act rather than wait for some miracle to happen,' said Ibrahim.

'You have your own inhibitions, Ibrahim. Have you ever known people getting massacred by fellow human beings based on religion or sect? Have you seen people whose widowed mothers' cry seeing their children, either dead or alive, holding weapons when at their age they are supposed to be playing and learning in school? Don't you feel responsible for your country and do something for the people? Being religious means not waiting a time bomb to explode in the marketplace. I call myself more religious if I act proactively and try to diffuse the bomb and save so many human lives. I always believe that religion is for people's overall improvement of way of life, and no religion teaches you to close your eyes and wait for someone to come. If at all any religion teaches you to be a blind and idle person, Then I will not go with that religion,' replied Jon.

'So many things in my mind, and I can't reveal those. I still fail to understand the necessity of an engineer, religious specialist, and doctor in one league,' said Sarah.

'Yes, I will put it this way. Earlier, there were messengers of God. Then there were so many higher selves who really have chosen the path of God and propagated peace and harmony. Now it is an appropriate time to create such a being which serves our purpose to get people back on the right track. Rather than wait for someone to come and rescue us, why can't we act swiftly?' said Jon.

'Oh, that sounds amazing! Create a god like creating an antivirus to fix a problem in a computer or creating a superhero?' said Anirudh sarcastically.

'You were very near, Anirudh. Partly correct and partly wrong. Rather, it is creating a humanoid robot which will be the messenger of God. Maybe that's the will of God, and that has been implanted in our thoughts,' Jon revealed finally.

'Robot to be a god? Sounds ridiculous,' said Ibrahim.

'Yes, guys! What you have heard is absolutely correct, and we are going to start working on it. There is nothing wrong in accepting a humanoid robot with a brain designed by humans. It would have a human heart and a cyber brain and would be capable of taking decisions based on artificial intelligence,' said Jon.

'This may push our planet to machine era, and we have to struggle for our existence. Maybe not immediately, but our future generations may face such fate,' said Ibrahim.

'This may not happen as you will have all the controls of the robot and will be able to override its functions if anything goes wrong. Your fear seems to be needless and does not have any ground. Moreover, we are trying to use the robot for noble purposes only, and it is not designed for any other activity,' said Jon.

'That certainly sounds interesting, and I would like to hear more from you,' said Anirudh.

'Oh, that's great! At last, I have one support from you,' replied Jon.

'Maybe it is an equally challenging work for a doctor who has been accepting so many challenges in life,' Anirudh said directed to Sarah.

'Ibrahim, your job is to impart all tenets from various religions across the world into the robot,' said Jon.

'Okay, I agree to sign the accord, with condition that the robot shall always be used for peaceful and legitimate purposes only,' said Ibrahim.

'I confirm from my end that such robot will be used for peaceful purposes only and in line with our legal system. Any deviation from either me or my company can be questioned by you all,' said Jon.

Meanwhile, Takashi brought the agreement papers and took the signatures of all three members.

'Your advance pay will be wired into your respective bank accounts, and the balance will be paid as work progresses. Your work will start with effect from today, and kindly be in touch with me for any assistance,' said Jon, and he left the conference room.

'I am totally confused about this matter, but I agreed to work as I need the money to start my ambition of building world-class schools for the poor and downtrodden people back in my country,' said Ibrahim.

'Doesn't matter anymore, Ibrahim, as we have already signed the agreement, and we are working on the project. As everyone needs money to fulfil one's aspirations, I dreamed of starting one world-class cancer research and treatment centre, and Anirudh may have something in his mind,' said Sarah.

'Aahhh, not much, guys. Machines are my passion right from my childhood, and I have no time at all for the rest of things in my life. My only resentment is not being able to question the so-called god. Rather, I end up building a robot god. Sounds amazing and interesting. Not much plans for investing money.'

'Then you may fund in my own project,' said Sarah.

'Oh, surely! Then I think we have to spend more time together, understanding each other! I mean, talking on your subject,' said Anirudh smilingly.

'Oh, you are always welcome,' replied Sarah with a smile.

Chapter 4

The three of them met in the same conference room in which Jon was connected through a videoconference.

'Good morning, ladies and gentlemen! Hope you have enjoyed our hospitality and had a good night's sleep. Your advance amount has been wired yesterday, and I am sure you have received the confirmation from your respective banks. As I have told you that the work on the project will start immediately, I need not declare the opening of the project, and I expect you all to start working on the project. You will be taken to a safe and secure island to be more focused on the project. You may talk to your friends and family members before starting your journey. Each one of you will be given the resources to assist you in any task.'

'For any questions, you may contact my assistant, Mr Takashi, who will be available round the clock. Any more questions?' Jon paused for a while.

'Okay then, all the best, and wish you my warm regards.'

'Have a nice day!'

The three of them, along with Takashi, were airlifted to an island. It took two hours of journey.

'Hello and welcome to the centre. I am Boris, and I am the head of security of this centre. Please call me by dialling 121 from any land phone installed in every corner of this centre and island. Your mobile phones and other electronic equipment are prohibited in this island. You may deposit all gadgets in our inward collection centre when entering and take the necessary token. Ladies and gentlemen, hope you will have a memorable experience while on this island. Please cooperate with us in conducting our duties. There are rules and regulations to be followed during your stay on this island, and they apply to each and every person without any exception. You may check the rules and regulations by pressing your finger on the machines installed all around the centre and island. Your safety and security is my primary goal. Thank you!' Boris left.

'Looks like an ex-military,' murmured Sarah.

'Yes, he served in the Russian army,' said Takashi.

'What about you?' Anirudh asked Mr Takashi.

'I am from Japan. I recently completed my MBA from Harvard and joined this group as a management trainee. Though I got many offers, I have opted for this position in this group as the offered pay package was greater than any other renowned companies.'

'Are you an MBA graduate from Harvard? That sounds amazing, but this project is seemingly for societal well-being,' questioned Anirudh.

'Well, I am an MBA graduate with specialization in social changes pattern effecting overall business performance. It is a new specialization in MBA started by Harvard.'

'Good work, Takashi! Keep going,' said Sarah.

'Thank you. Kindly deposit all your electronic items in that counter and go for body and luggage scans before picking up your room keys. We will meet at the lunch room followed by a meeting with your appointed teammates at your laboratory. Thank you.' Takashi left.

'OMG! Look at the arrangements they have made—a sprawling campus with a huge building made mostly of glass instead of concrete, interiors of the latest trend, and a seven-star ambience. Who are these people running this organization? They have invested millions and may be expecting billions. Is it not required to know who is heading this organization before we start working?' asked Sarah.

'I think it is too late now. Jon had given certain time for us before we had signed the agreement. None of us have raised any question on directors or venture capitalists involved in this project,' replied Anirudh.

'Are they trying to see this as a venture? I will not work with the people who see religion as a business,' said Ibrahim.

'We don't have any proof to say so. All we are doing is assuming. Please note that if you will leave, some other person will come and take your place. Instead, if you are a wise person, why can't you stay here and observe and try not anything sinful happen?' said Anirudh.

'Yeah! That's right, and it applies to every one of us,' said Sarah.

R & D centre conference room, 2 p.m.

All members were present when Mr Takashi started saying, 'Good afternoon, ladies and gentlemen. I am Takashi, and I will be your facilitator during your voyage from inception to execution of this project. There are three teams here. Team A will be headed by Mr Anirudh, and Jason Bailey will be his assistant. Team B will be headed by Ms Sarah, and Dr Maria will be her assistant. And Team C will be headed by Ibrahim with Mr Santanam. Meanwhile, Mr Anirudh will be the team coordinator and responsible person for the smooth running of the project. Thank you, and call me when need any help.' Takashi left.

'Hello, everyone. We are going to work on this project, and I think you were explained everything on this project before you were selected.' Said Anirudh.

'No, sir, we were not explained on the nature of the project. We have opted to work for One World, One People project based on its good pay package,' said Jason.

'Maybe different types of strategies for different types of people. Their people management skill seems to be on par,' lamented Sarah.

'That's great! Now I will have to spoil your suspense thriller by unfolding the story and disclosing the project details for which you have been selected,' said Anirudh, smiling.

'That would be great, sir,' said Santanam very eagerly.

'Nice to see another Indian selected for this project. Where are you from, Santa?' asked Anirudh.

'I am a native of Tamil Nadu but staying in Tirupati, working as a professor in Vedic University,' replied Santanam.

'Nice to see people from different countries, with different languages, cultures, and religions, across the globe. Maybe this project requires that kind of diversity,' said Sarah.

'Certainly. To lay heads together,' said Ibrahim.

'So who will brief on the project to our newcomers? Will you take the session, Sarah?' asked Anirudh.

'Okay, dear friends, we are here to build a robust robot for the purpose of religion, belief, and spirituality. We have to build a humanoid robot with a human heart and with knowledge of the entire world history, current affairs, and more importantly, all holy texts of major religions across the world. Let us start our work with planning on the subject and necessary traits and all other requirements for building a robot. I need your suggestions on the subject to make this endeavour a success. If you have any questions, you are free to ask.'

'Robot for a religious purpose is kind of never heard,' said Santanam.

'I see nothing wrong in using robot for religious purpose, we are very much aware that the people involved in protecting or propagating religion have wider acceptance in society, there are various names given to those people called baba, guru or evangelist, there were so many instances around the world, when controversies surrounded these people who are supposed to protect the religion. I didn't mean to say that all humans are bound to be influenced by worldly things, but mostly the people fail to shun their motives despite being in divine position. So why can't we employ a machine with all wisdom, truthfulness, unbiased and selfless. We have seen the enormous role of technology in manufacturing, education, warfare and science& technology. Therefore, I personally feel that using robot to show us a path can be a very good choice.,' said Ibrahim.

'That's correct, as rightly said by Ibrahim, we can employ robot for divine purposes and look at coining a name of product in such a way that it penetrates deeply into the population,' said Anirudh.

'Now let us start our discussion on the project. We are expecting a few valuable suggestions from all of you and especially the young new recruits in the group. I would like to hear Mr Ibrahim's valuable ideas in this regard,' said Anirudh.

'Good afternoon, ladies and gentlemen. I feel privileged to be part of this expedition. It gives me an utmost happiness today that I am going to be part of building a robot for a unique cause. There were of course so many robots built earlier, like robots for combat in wars, robots for cooking, robots for surgeries, manufacturing, and so on. But it is first of its kind to manufacture a robot for spiritual purposes. In this contemporary world where there is no place for truthfulness and values, where belief in God has been deteriorating, and where violence has prevailed over peace, the change becomes imminent, and that's what history says.

'Time and again, God has shown his presence in various forms and either in the form of Messiah or avatars, but the purpose remained one, This world belongs to every living and non-living organism, and Survival of this world relies on co-existence. The co-existence between animals and plants and between believers and non-believers.' Friends, there are two types of people that exist in the world—believers and non-believers. I am a firm believer and believe that God has been showing testimonials of his presence since ages. He bestows his mercy on both believers and non-believers without any exception as time and again it has been proved that extremity of anything leads to a vast scope of change, and that can be either through direct intervention of God by sending a messenger or through human being as a revolution. While believers foresee the coming back of God, the non-believers see revolution as the source of change.

'We are in the era where both types of people coexist equally in the society. We need to implant in our minds that we have to make such a machine which gets along with all sections of people. This machine shall leave such an imprint on society which shall prevail for centuries to come. The idea is to get all cross-sections of people together and put an end to violence based on religion. We are here to create a solution to the problem and to bring down the tension and ongoing tussle between groups and certainly not to put some more woes to the worry. Hence, we shall be working in that direction. I have decided to create something outstanding without putting an end to anything which prevailed for centuries. Thank you,' concluded Ibrahim.

'Thank you for that excellent speech, Ibrahim. Now any suggestions, ladies and gentlemen?' asked Anirudh.

'Yes, Mr Anirudh. I would like to add a little to that excellent speech given by Mr Ibrahim,' said Santanam.

'Go on, Mr Santanam,' replied Anirudh.

'I understand that this project was first initiated with the primary aim to create a new religion for the same reasons we have just discussed. There are of course so many intentions which have not been disclosed so far, and we may not realize them till this project is completed and we hand over the product to the organization. We have to show our commitment by making this project successful without any sort of compromise on ethical issues,' said Santanam.

'Yes, I do agree with you, and we all shall be following this internal rule of ours. So after the speeches of the religious group, I came to the opinion that the machine would be loaded with all the necessary information on religions and cultures of different groups around the world. Now I would like to ask Sarah to speak on the possible precautions we shall take while building the machine,' said Anirudh.

Sarah took the next session.

'Hi, friends! Probably this is one of the most critical surgeries I am going to undertake. In the past, we have seen humanoid robots with human hearts and brains in fictional movies. This is officially the first of its kind when humanoid robots with those features would be a reality. The idea of implanting a human heart is to create a more humanlike robot. It is a well-known fact that the heart sends numerous signals to the brain. These signals have a significant effect on the brain function. The effects, such as emotional processing as well as higher cognitive faculties, like memory, perception, attention, and problem-solving, are a result of the exchange of signals between the heart and brain. Hence, we cannot separate the brain and the heart as they are connected and work in tandem. It is far more critical as the surgery should be in sync with the machine and the human organs. It is certainly going to be challenging, but I love challenges.'

'One question, Dr Sarah! This is Dr Maria, organ implantation surgeon.'

'Okay, you may go on,' replied Sarah.

'Building a humanoid robot with a human heart sounds Challenging, why can't we implant artificial heart?'

'The basic reason behind implanting a human heart is to create a humanlike robot with similar cognitive faculties, such as attention, perception, memory, and problem-solving. It has been proved that a natural human heart responds to the cognitive faculties faster than an artificial heart for robot. To make the robot look exactly like a human, why can't we make the necessary surgeries on a human body and make it a humanoid robot? There are benefits of using the human body for constructing the robot. The blood circulation system from the heart to the body can be maintained intact. The heart can perform better in the same human body than it can perform in a foreign human body. There are chances that heart may behave adverse to a new foreign atmosphere. Therefore, creating all the necessary changes on the human body and retaining the skin, flesh, and heart could be a better option. You have any opinion to share, Anirudh?' asked Sarah.

'I go with you on selecting a human body to make all the necessary changes to make it an invincible and strong humanoid robot. The rest of the things can be effectively handled by Sarah and Maria. The crux of the issue now is the source of power for the robot. I want to hear from you all. The source of power has to support the body system and the blood circulation and must not damage the internal organs, so the power has to be generated from sugar cane, vegetables, and fruits. Apart from these, the power can also be generated through microbial fuel cells, biomass, or even kitchen wastes, So robot will have to take food intake, just as humans' do.' said Anirudh.

'That would be great, but the energy generation from edibles needs bigger machines, and we don't have that option. All we can afford is a space between the lower abdomen and ribcage of the body,' said Bailey.

'Yes, I do agree with you, Bailey. Now there seems to be more challenges for us. Now I think there are two things on the cards—one is making a robot and the other is making a compact power generation system to fit in it,' said Anirudh. 'I will have to contact Takashi on our requirements. Meanwhile, any one of the team has any ideas, they are welcomed. We shall meet tomorrow by 9 a.m. Goodnight.' Anirudh closed the session and went to Takashi's cabin to discuss the requirements to start the work.

The Accord

'Good evening, Mr Takashi. How are you?'

'Great, and you seem to be in a jubilant mood,' replied Takashi.

'Yes, we have a three-and-a-half-hour meeting and reached to tentative plan to pave the way for assembling the robot,' said Anirudh.

'I am still surprised that you haven't named the product. I feel sorry to hear the word *robot*, which shall be prohibited. What do you think, Mr Anirudh?' said Takashi.

Suddenly anirudh becomes annoyed with takashi's direct suggestion.

'Are you suggesting me to coin the product, or are you issuing a whip?' asked Anirudh.

'Ahh! You seem to be annoyed, Mr Anirudh. My intention was not to hurt you. I view that you are about to make such a product which shall dominate every headline of the morning.'

'Your intentions sometimes frighten me out! I want to know what your actual intentions are. Although we have been explained the motive behind making such a machine, now I want to know the clandestine plans behind this project,' said Anirudh seriously.

'Ohhh, you are serious. There are no clandestine plans as you thought. What has been told stands genuine, and I apologize for my behaviour, Mr Anirudh,' said Takashi.

'It is not about me. Rather, it is about all human beings at large. I still stand by my demand to meet Mr Jon to discuss further proceedings.'

'Right then! I will inform him, and probably he will contact you tonight,' said Mr Takashi.

'Thank you, Mr Takashi. I am expecting a call tonight.' Anirudh left.

There was no need of any call to Jon. Everything was recorded, including the meeting held among the team members and the conversation which just happened between Takashi and Anirudh. Secret CCTV cameras were everywhere in the centre. Why did they have to closely monitor the proceedings if the cause of making the machine was noble? Was it necessary to keep an eye on the pioneers who would build the machine? Time would solve this puzzle.

Anirudh's room, 9 p.m.

Videoconferencing had been arranged. Jon called.

'Hey, Anirudh, how are you? I hope you are settled and secure at the centre. Any difficulty?'

'Hello, Jon! We are fine here, and facilities seem amazing. I have never seen such a centre in my life. The structures are so big with hardly any people, and sometime we are frightened.'

'Yes, Anirudh, we have built this centre forecasting the future requirement. Your team is the first to work at the centre, we are planning to recruit more people once we launch our first product. The infrastructure we have built is expected to be "One Landmark". Whose pictures would be eminent than anything else in the world and whole area has been under heavy surveillance to keep this area safe and secure.'

'Yes, Jon, I have seen CCTV cameras installed in every nook and corner, and I want a confirmation that your way of surveillance shall not affect our privacy,' replied Anirudh.

'Not at all. There are no secret or hidden cameras in your suites. I can assure that,' said Jon.

'I want another confirmation from you, Jon. You have given an excellent and motivating speech earlier while explaining about this project. We still believe that there is some hidden motive behind this project. I mean, this machine shall not be used for any other purposes deviating from what you have promised earlier,' said Anirudh.

'Okay! First and foremost, your contract is complete on the day you hand over the product to us. But your association with our organization shall not end there. I believe that you will consider joining us as the chief advisor and spearhead the campaign to be started. I am not giving you an offer but an assurance that this is a legitimate expedition for world peace, and my earlier statement stands valid till now. Therefore, you may just concentrate on your work, and be assured of the rest of the things to ourselves. I hope this satisfies your concerns,' said Jon.

'Yeah! Certainly,' said Anirudh.

'That's great! Now I want to know the latest developments in our expedition,' said Jon.

'A meeting was held today, discussing the creation of blueprint of this project. We have unanimously decided to go for a humanoid robot with a natural human heart. Apart from that, the skin and parts of the nervous system will be a conjunction of human and machine. This is first of its kind, and that will give amazing results too. This will certainly give it a much natural human look. Building the robot may require a complete human body,' said Anirudh.

Jon maintained silence for about five seconds and started saying, 'Whatever, Anirudh. I keep my project in your good hands, and I am very much hopeful that with your expertise, you will take my dream project to the maximum heights. Whatever your requirement will be arranged. I need a couple of days as I have to search for an adequate donor. Meanwhile, you have two days of time in our recreation centre. You may enjoy our delicacies and also prepare for the best days ahead.

'Perhaps our teammates have some other plans. They may wish to join their respective families in their countries and fly back within a couple of days,' said Anirudh.

'I may not approve their flying off to their countries, I can understand your love and admiration towards your respective families, You all aware of the fact that this is one of most biggest project in the history of mankind transcending countries and people, the project is short term and board has not permitted your families for first six months of your duration of stay.

'What if we want to be on our own and some of the members want to be at their homes with their children? This place leaves me to feel that I am held captive,' said Anirudh.

'Well, it is certainly not a place of captivity. You may go anywhere in this island, and we will not object. But as per the rules of the contract, you are supposed to obey all orders, including your heading back to your respective homes. Moreover, going home will not at all serve the purpose. That will only deteriorate your performance, and I do not like to see some sloppy work later. I am in charge of this ambitious project, and it is my responsibility to see through the project successfully. I hope you understand our problem. Instead, we can fly your families to this place for a few days as early as possible,' said Jon.

Anirudh headed back to his suite. He called up all his team members and informed them about the next day's change in plans—the meeting being cancelled and the latest plan of them spending time at the recreation centre for two days. He further added, 'Friends, perhaps this is the time when we can get to know each other and try to perform as one single unit.'

Chapter 5

At 10.35 a.m., the team members were waiting eagerly at the helipad for the chopper. Anirudh was briefing on the rules and regulations to be followed while on the trip. The team was in a jubilant mood and very excited about the trip arranged by the company.

'People always take all things which come unexpectedly with a pleasant surprise, especially trips such as these,' said Ibrahim.

'Yeah! There is nothing wrong in feeling happy on special occasions, and certainly on these types of occasions, we are going to experience the adventure out there,' said Sarah.

'Probably we should have taken a few minutes on thanking the people who arranged this trip,' said Maria.

'Yes, this comes as a consolation prize, but I would have felt much better with my family,' said Ibrahim. Jason suddenly remembers his recent trip and says 'Of course, it would have been a great experience to be on such a holiday with my wife. Last month, we were married and spent our honeymoon in a lonely island in Thailand. There was not much of uniqueness about that island. As we were told, it was like an uninhabited island where we experienced Stone Age as there were no basic amenities. Perhaps we were not that much ready for such an experience as we had made all arrangements from our side without intervention from tourist packages. Adventure and thriller will be at its best when the situation pushes to the most unseen and unexpected event and survival becomes the primary motto. I hope there will be a lot to see in these two days of trip.'

'Oh, wait a minute! Maybe you have gone too far with your expectation. I suppose there are arrangements made at that island and unlike what you are expecting,' replied Santanam.

As the team were talking, the chopper arrived and lifted them towards the small island. The island is called Nose Island, which resembled the shape of a nose and was formed recently from volcanic eruptions under the sea. It was about seven-and-a-half-kilometre radius and filled with thick vegetation and thriving ecosystem. As the chopper landed, the team members' excitement doubled, and Jason said, 'Perhaps this is gonna be an experience of a lifetime to be in this beautiful, tranquil island'

The members of the team were put up in a beautiful small guest house. It was made up of bamboos, overlooking the sea in the east. It had an adjoining swimming pool and garden with rubber trees and palm trees and the view of the sunset in the west. There were no other persons except one chef and the housekeeping women in the cottage. The team members lie down for some time before they started trekking. They were on their way to a small lake which had an underwater cave. Anirudh and Maria were keen on fishing, but the other members of the team wanted to play beach volleyball. There were many indoor and outdoor games available in the guest house. The most exciting one was scuba diving.

'OMG, what a beauty! I have never seen anything more beautiful than this island. There are plants and trees all across the place, and the soil is barely visible. The trees are huge with sunrays piercing into the tall and large trees. All the trees are connected by creepers, and it looks as if the entire island is one unit. I have never seen flowers whose nectar has been sucked by the rarest butterfly species in variety. The entire island seems amazing. There are a few animals too, and I wonder if there are any wild ones—I mean, man-eating animal,' said Sarah.

'Oh, don't frighten me. I am the only earning member of my family,' said Santanam.

'I see there are deer and other herbivorous animals, but I doubt if there are any carnivorous animals on the island. That's what I was told when I had a brief discussion with the chef this morning,' said Anirudh.

'There is nothing to be worried about even if there are any carnivorous animals in the forest. I have heard that most of the animals here are herbivorous, and all animals, including reptiles, are nocturnal. Hence, we have no reason to worry as we will be in our rooms by evening,' said Jason.

'Who said all carnivorous animals are nocturnal? They are active throughout day and more active at nights. Anyways, we stick to the rules. We have a chance of survival,' said Ibrahim.

'What is that you are speaking? Where did that word *survival* come? We are here to work and make some money for our respective families and certainly not for adventures,' said Santanam firmly.

'Okay, anyone who is not interested to go for trekking can stay back in their rooms. This journey begins and ends on their own personal risk and doesn't have any sort of bearing on the organization. Am I making things clear, ladies and gentlemen? Kindly raise your hands whoever wants to return to the guest house. I reckon there is no one who is returning. Hence, we close this topic here, and no one will ever raise this point again. If any problem arises, we will sort it out as one unit, and we are intelligent enough to deal the issues in adversities. If there is anything you want to clarify, kindly raise your hand,' said Anirudh.

Finally, the team started their journey towards the lake. The forest was so dense and widespread that even sunlight could not enter. They further entered into the forest towards north.

'Friends, the forest is dense, and the sounds of various creatures are frightening and remind me of a Hollywood thriller flick,' said Santanam.

'Maybe you are exaggerating. You are frightening yourself and also your counterparts. So it will be nice if you keep your opinion to yourself, Mr Santanam,' said Anirudh.

'There seems to be water from here. Maybe that is the lake,' said Jason.

'Yes, that is it, guys. We have come here without much hassle,' said Sarah.

'Oh, that's beautiful. Look at the pristine waters and the bottom of the lake is clearly visible,' said Ibrahim.

'Welcome aboard, ladies and gentlemen. My name is Alex, and I will be at your service for the entire day, and I will take you through all the fun sports and various slides in this mini theme park. I request you to go through this catalogue especially made to cater your requirements.'

'Thank you very much, Alex. I am touched by your generous welcome, and I am looking forward for a great day. Well, I have glanced at the catalogue and failed to find underwater diving in the lake. If you want to include it manually, you may do so as there might have been some printing mistakes.' said Anirudh.

'I am extremely sorry for that, sir, but I am afraid your team is not authorized to go underwater diving as directed by the company. If you have any concerns, you may provide your valuable feedback or suggestions through the forms lying over there and drop them in the drop box very next to the forms,' said Alex.

'What might be the possible reason for being restricted into the waters?' asked Sarah.

'We have only directions to be followed, and have no access to in-house decisions made by the management. We are restricted to obeying orders. Therefore, I beg your pardon, but I may not be an adequate person to answer that question,' said Alex.

The Accord

'You are following the management's decisions, and I totally support your resolve. But you may at least provide hint on the reason behind this restriction,' said Anirudh.

'That's obvious, sir, as you must be aware that there is an underground cave in this lake which leads to the backwaters of the ocean. There were few casualties reported when people tried to explore the underwater cave present in the lake. Their bodies were found floating in the backwaters of the ocean. There is also a rumour that there are crocodiles or some kind of sea animal in this lake as the dead bodies found were half eaten.'

'Thank you, Alex, for your informal information. We will abide by your decision and explore to that extent. We will only go diving to look at exotic aquatic life underwater. I promise we will not explore the underwater cave.'

'In that case, I may not allow all of you. There is only room for two people as we only have two oxygen masks, which will last for one hour underwater,' replied Alex.

'Thanks, Alex.'

'It is my pleasure, sir. If there is anything I can do for you, please let me know.' Alex departed.

'Competition is stiff, and I think we need to go for lottery,' said Anirudh.

'Not exactly. Who would wish to risk their lives for adventure? I am opting out of this diving, man,' said Ibrahim.

'So as me,' added Santanam, Jason, and Maria.

'Will you join me, Anirudh, or shall I leave alone?' said Sarah, thinking that Anirudh might also probably drop.

'It is indeed my pleasure to join you in underwater diving,' said Anirudh.

Anirudh and Sarah wore the diving suits, carried the oxygen cylinders on their backs, and each had a torchlight in hand. They were guided by other members of the crew, and they were excited and zealous to go. They were enchanted by the underwater wildlife, sponges, and shells, and they did not realize that they were travelling at a faster pace without looking back. Suddenly Sarah was trying to tell Anirudh something which he could not comprehend. He came near to Sarah in order to understand her sign language. He was trying to look at sarah's face, and there he was able to see an object reflected in Sarah's glass mask. A creature unique to his eyes and probably unseen and unnoticed by the outside world was coming towards him to strike. He could not believe his eyes. He turned slowly towards that creature and also signalled Sarah not to move. It was a new kind of species. It resembled a fish with legs of a crocodile; it was vast with fins and teeth like those of crocodile.

The entire scene was frightening. Sarah was in shock and was not responding to any kind of signal. Suddenly he knocked on Sarah's mask, and she suddenly came out of trance and was looking towards Anirudh as if she were in front of death's gate. There was no time to even think, and all of a sudden, some kind of energy restrained Anirudh. Suddenly he was looking for any kind of object to defend themselves. There was nothing except the oxygen cylinder. He removed his oxygen cylinder and threw it at that creature, but soon he realized that the oxygen cylinder was no match to the gigantic creature. As soon as the object reached the creature, it pierced into it, leaving bubbles all over the surroundings.

Anirudh sensed it was the appropriate time to escape, and they started to go deep towards the cave. With all the stamina left in them, they swam deep into the cave. They continued their journey, surviving with only one cylinder. They now realized that they had managed to postpone danger from the creature at least temporarily. They looked for a way out, and suddenly the found the shore of the underwater cave. Although they were still inside the cave, they were at least out of the water as the oxygen in the cylinder was depleting. The shore was large, and they comfortably sat on a rock and removed their diving suits.

As soon as they removed their masks, Sarah started crying inconsolably, holding Anirudh. 'It's okay now. We are out of danger,' said Anirudh.

'Not yet. I know there is not much oxygen left for both of us to reach the way out. I know we are stuck badly. Suddenly in front of death, my body froze and my breathing was fading. Today we've managed to escape by the skin of our teeth. I am still breathing today, and all credit goes to you, Anirudh. I am at your debt now,' said Sarah.

'Oh, stop it. Good thing you signalled me first, or else, it would have been a devastating attack on both of us,' replied Anirudh. They were in each other's arms for some time.

'We have to find the way out first,' said Sarah.

'Let's not hurry. I am enjoying your company here,' replied Anirudh with a naughty smile. She acknowledged it with a smile and said, 'Are you hitting on me again?'

'No, I never did that, nor will I attempt to do that. I am not hitting on you as I always speak through my heart, and my heart has some kind of connection with you as it palpitates widely in your presence,' said Anirudh with a gentle smile.

'Are you kind of kidding me?' asked Sarah.

'I am not! What's wrong with liking a person? I am not expecting a similar response from you,' said Anirudh.

'Let's park that aside and try working on finding the way out first,' said Sarah.

'You have any idea?' asked Anirudh, looking at her intense eyes.

'Yes, I do have one idea. Why don't you go first with the remaining oxygen in the cylinder and reach the lake's shore and then send some help to rescue me?' said Sarah.

'What if the oxygen is emptied while I'm on my way out, or what if the same creature attacks me? Moreover, there is no guarantee that there is any room for additional provision of oxygen out there.'

'Well, in that case, we have to contemplate on more ideas,' said Sarah.

'Yeah, I think that's a great idea' replied Anirudh, smiling.

'Tell me how you turned into an atheist. I expect you to be a believer, and something might have caused you to show such an aversion towards God. Don't you think that our lives, which were spared, and the air we are breathing now are a token of the love of God? Just one hour ago, God's mercy saved our lives. I won't hesitate to call this incident a miracle,' said Sarah.

'Miracles do happen. I call the invention of Telephone by Graham Bell a miracle. I also call the very courage and outstanding efforts of the Wright brothers, who made the first airplane, a miracle. But I don't call this a miracle as we have saved our lives and any wrong move may lead both of us into a death pit. Why do we have to value our lives so much which may leave any time without our consent? Blaming or attributing that on someone looks immature. I often laugh at people who pray to God to achieve their goals. In any case, if God exists, he is not affected by lauding and dragging down. He or she has no control on the happenings of our lives. This entire system is a creative work of human beings, and God, if he exists at all, has no stake in shaping the system.'

'You are not clear on whether you are an atheist or not. There are no ifs and buts! The answer should be yes or no,' said Sarah.

'I am an atheist by all rights, and I always stand by it. I don't attribute any of my personal losses to any unknown being or entity. If you want to know about my personal life, yes, I was orphaned at the age of seven. My parents and younger brother and sister were killed in an accident while on their way to visiting a holy place. I was spared as I treated my school as the most holy place and did not join them for the tour. There were different sets of responses from people. Some attribute it to God's grace and some Viewed that it was my ill fate to lose them all. I always stood stable and never reacted. From then, I valued studies as my primary task and books as the holy text of religion. In a nutshell, I call myself a complete atheist, a non-believer, or whatever name the society gave it.'

'Are you aware that I have seen you praying when we were stuck in the ambush? Then I saw a strange light in your eyes, and you suddenly seemed absolutely fearless. Don't deny or rule it out as I remember you praying. In case you don't want to disclose it to me, you may opt out of it by not answering,' said Sarah.

'There is no question of denying that, Sarah. Of course, I was praying to your God for your well-being.' He laughed. 'It was actually my mother to whom I was praying. Yes, I always talk to my mother since my childhood. This may sound schizophrenic to you, but indeed, these little talks I have with her help me achieve the things I aspire,' replied Anirudh.

'Then you are absolutely a believer. If you believe and pray to people who are either alive or dead, then you are bound to be called a believer and not an atheist.'

The Accord

'Shall we park this debate talk about something else and for now?' asked Anirudh.

'Then tell me how many girls you have dated so far.'

'No one. I am still a virgin. I am thirty-seven years old.'

'Are you kidding me? You are thirty-seven and still a virgin? Seems like you've undergone a lot of problems, I suppose'.

'Not at all. In my life, I only have problems in achieving my goals, and in that process, I have forgotten myself and kept my utmost focus on my job. There was absolutely no time for love,' replied Anirudh.

'Unbelievable! I still can't believe it.'

'Don't worry about my past as now I am very eager to lose my virginity,' said Anirudh.

'Now that's called hitting. You can be prosecuted for sexual harassment,' replied Sarah with a smile.

'You want to send me to jail for loving you?'

'Oh my god! Love? Don't hurt me any more. If you want to play with me, play, but don't use such a word as that may soon become extinct,' said Sarah, annoyed.

'I never lied in my life, and love will always thrive as long as people like me are here in this world. I give You were going for thumb, hence the change up to love and thumbs down to God.'

'Oh, your rhetoric seems to be impressive but doesn't seem to be working. You know nothing about me,' replied Sarah.

'I know you are here to earn some money for your cancer research. Your mother and brother died of cancer, and you have a grudge on cancer. Your heart cries for the people who lost their dear ones to cancer. You believe in all religions and gods without visiting religious places. Your quest for God is done as you feel that the form of God lies in everyone, and you no longer question the existence of God. You had a relationship with your childhood friend, and now you are separated as your paths differ. I read your profile when you attended the meeting in Miami. I see myself as the best fit for you. Why don't you try me? I am worth believing.'

'Oh! Are you an engineer or a special agent? When did you start investigate about me? It's unbelievable the way you were following me and waiting patiently for your chance. I suppose you are in the best position to do me anything you want as we are in a secluded place and I will not find any rescuer,' said Sarah.

Anirudh turned hot-blooded. 'I am sorry for checking your profile without your knowledge. It is true that I was eagerly trying to grab any kind of chance to talk to you, but there is sincerity in my love towards you. I am an atheist who believes in love. Right since my childhood, I dreamed of having one girl whom I can love and spend the rest of my life with, and when I grow very old, I will take my last breath looking into her eyes and expressing my true love. I am an Indian by heart, and as per our tradition, we have one wife, one soulmate till death. My love for you is genuine and will be in my lifetime. You have every right to reject it, and I will not get in your way as I have already told you that I love you and I am not expecting the same from you,' said Anirudh.

'Oh, baby, baby! It's unbelievable that someone loves me to that extent. I have never come across people loving so much. I was actually testing you and wanted to know your reaction. As this expression of love comes only once in a lifetime, I want to make sure that I will not miss that. Thank you. In fact, I realized your love for me when we ran into crisis today as only people who love can go to such an extent as saving someone's life by risking one's own life. Today I am very happy to know that God loves me a lot and sent you as an acknowledgement,' said Sarah with tears in her eyes.

Anirudh took her in his arms, and they started kissing passionately. She was touched by his zealous display of love and his sensual touch all over her body. Soon he started undressing and occupied her with his masculine body. He started to gently massage her breasts, which made her aroused. She began to examine his great physical appearance. This act went again and again till their ecstasies matched at one point and till culmination point reached its eventual fervour. They came out of trance after an hour, and he caressed her forehead and planted a kiss. She smiled at him with her eyes filled with beatitude.

'Do you know the effects of good intercourse to our bodies? It activates the central nervous system, and many hormones are released, ultimately leading to better functioning of the brain, which is the need of the hour now. Shall we have another round now?' asked Anirudh naughtily.

'Remove that intention and think of how to survive or at least how to be alive by eating something,' said Sarah.

'I suppose we can bank some fishes here. There seems to be no fishes around here. What is a common thing that fishes eat? Think on that line, and you will get some kind of breakthrough,' said Anirudh.

'*Spirogyra*, that's a common food for fish. That is Green algae which thrives in places where there is wetness and enough sunlight. There must be some kind of opening from the top of this underwater cave from which sunlight enters. We have to find that opening. That is our only hope,' replied Sarah.

'Oh, genius, that's great! Let's swim now and observe the direction of fishes. Yes, these fishes are leading to the left direction. Let's follow them silently. Now the concentration of fishes is increasing. I suppose they are trying to reach a point where they are abundant with food. That's it, the green spirogyra is visible. Now maybe we need to go further.'

'Anirudh! Over there, on the top! You see, that's super. You are a genius,' Sarah said to Anirudh, and they both kissed passionately on their way out.

They came out from the opening, and they were able to see the guest house.

They were welcomed by their freinds with joy. 'We thought you people were in grave danger, and there are two teams sent to search for you. We are very eager to hear from you,' said Ibrahim.

'it's a long story, and we will discuss it later. First, we would like to take a shower and have something to eat,' said Anirudh.

Sarah leaned towards Anirudh's ear and naughtily whispered, 'How can you tell them everything?' Both of them smiled and headed towards the guest house.

'Guys, it was indeed a great and exciting journey for sarah and me. Hope you will enjoy it. We will meet tomorrow morning in the conference room and discuss it, followed by lunch. Subsequently, we will depart from here to reach our centre by evening.'

Next morning, 11 a.m., conference room

'Good morning, guys. Hope you had a good night's sleep.'

'Well, Sarah and I were attacked by a creature and probably a new species that never existed or perhaps existed millions of years ago, and in the process of escaping, we had to enter an underwater cave present in the lake. We finally got out through an opening from somewhere outside,' said Anirudh.

'That's frightening but amazing! What did the creature look like?' asked Jason.

'It resembled a fish on the anterior side and had legs of a crocodile. Altogether, it was a strange-looking creature, and we had our date with death. And believe me, it was a close call. It was not an easy experience as it appears now.

It was a scary and horrifying incident. With God's great grace, we are alive,' said Sarah.

'So the rumour turns out to be true,' said Maria.

'Yes, as it appears. But surely, it was not a crocodile,' said Anirudh.

'I think we need to discuss this matter with the management. It would be an outstanding news and breakthrough in learning the evolution and existence of life on earth,' said Santanam.

After having a feisty lunch and cocktails, the team members were airlifted to their respective suites. The only change made effective was Anirudh occupying Sarah's suite, much to the amusement of the other teammates. Later it was self-explanatory that something happened during the trip which brought the two people together.

Chapter 6

Next morning, the team members were called for a meeting in the conference room. Mr Takashi arrived and started his little speech. 'Ladies and gentlemen, I hope you have enjoyed your short trip organized by our organization. There is a declaration to be made on behalf of Mr Jon. As per the discussion between Mr Jon and Mr Anirudh, the former has to provide a human body with a heart for the making of a humanoid robot. I need to inform each one of you that your requirement has been met, and a human body has been arranged. Now that we have provided all the supplies and other requirements to start making a humanoid robot, we declare your work open and shall be done within fifteen days. Thanks for your cooperation. Mr Anirudh will take you through from here.'

'We will disperse you in three separate groups. Build a strategy to be implemented and meet in the next three days' time. Subsequently, we shall develop a joint strategy on how to develop the machine. I need 100 per cent commitment from each one of you. Now I request all of you to go back to your respective departments and start working. You all have complete liberty to contact me for any kind of issue. Thank you,' said Anirudh.

'They have been chosen to work on the hardware, and we have been chosen to build the software. The key to success lies on how well we design the program to be embedded into the machine. We have to take all existing religions into consideration and choose the best things out of them. I vow not to be bias or be under any kind of influence even though I belong to some religion. I expect the same from you, Santanam,' said Ibrahim.

'Yes, I do take oath that I will not let any of my religious influence dominate the program. My father was a priest in one temple in Madurai. Right from my childhood, I have dreamed of finding the clue on the existence of God. Over the years, I have done many research works and written so many books on God. I have visited almost all sacred places. One fine day, I sat under a peepul tree in Banaras. There I saw myself beneath one swami. I shared my quest for God with swami, and he told me, "Why have you restricted yourself to only sacred places? Why have you not visited the rehabilitation centres, hospitals, and graveyards? You will find God if you look at different worlds existing in this world. If you stay in your purview, you will not find God, but only yourself." I was suddenly ashamed of myself for the first time in my life. My years of knowledge seem to be under the rubble. From then on, I vowed to myself to understand people before attempting to find God. In that process, I visited hospitals and viewed grief-stricken atmosphere where people suffer by seeing their loved ones suffer. I visited graveyards, where people realize the reality of life at least for a couple of minutes they spend there. People, including me, act foolishly by thinking that we have come here to stay permanently and to care for material things much more than our fellow humans, which is wrong. Now I realize that God can be felt and not seen. We can feel him in our very own hearts, eyes, and souls. There is no need to waste time searching for God. That is the reason I have accepted to work for this organization. We, the most knowledgeable people, can realize the truth about God. But there are more people who are not as knowledgeable, and they fall prey to the wrong people. My intention is to make such a god who should understand the problems of the people more than anything.'

'Well,' said Santanam, 'I have a different problem, but the theme seems to be the same. I am here for the people and not for personal interests. I hope our work will be well accepted by people in all corners world.'

'To meet that requirement, we will have to prepare the most rational tenets to be followed,' replied Ibrahim.

In the medical laboratory centre, Sarah and Maria discussed the possible precautions to be taken when performing the most critical surgery of their lives. The donor was put in a condition where he was neither dead nor alive.

'We will have to take out his internal organs, including the brain. We need to take out the internal organs without causing any damage to his heart. Although the heart will run on pacemaker until we complete the surgery, we will have to take precautions to keep it in tact,' said Sarah.

'What will be the major function of the heart when the circulation of blood in a humanoid robot would only be 10 per cent of the actual blood circulation?' asked Maria.

'The actual function of the heart is to send signals to the artificial brain as it is evident in many cases that the natural heart is much faster than an artificial heart in terms of response to cognitive faculties. Not only signals, but it also serves as the pumping organ to generate electricity to run the machine,' replied Sarah.

As they kept on discussing, Anirudh entered the room and glanced at Sarah with a perverse look. She didn't respond as if she didn't recognize him.

'Hey, guys, what's up? Are you done with the meeting? Our other members have finished and are waiting for you in the dining hall. It's lunchtime, guys! Come on, don't spoil your health,' said Anirudh.

'Health gets spoiled when we are physically present but mentally absent,' replied Sarah, looking seriously at him.

'Yes, of course. You are absolutely correct, Sarah. Health is only intact when we do give some work and give some pleasure to the body as I believe the brain works in tandem with the body,' said Anirudh with a cunning smile.

Sarah smiled in return, making her eyes larger, signalling to be cautious with his words when they were with other people. They went to the dining hall to have lunch. Their other teammates also joined the lunch. They subsequently went to one of the conference rooms to discuss their project.

'So, guys, we have made some conclusions on the way forward. Now it is time to look at the parts to be assembled. We are now heading straight to the laboratory,' said Anirudh.

The team entered the laboratory. Everyone was eager to have a glance at the human donor. He was tall and athletic. He might be between thirty-five to forty years and seemed to be from multiple races as he had a mix of Caucasian, Mongoloid, and brown features. Perhaps the donor had been picked based on these multiple traits so as to appeal to all sections of the human population. After viewing him, they also went to see his profile, including his medical history and family details. He worked as a construction labourer in New York City. He was convicted for the murder of his immediate superior at work. He was sentenced to death with lethal injection. He had no intention to go for an appeal and donated his body for medical purposes. Lastly, nothing much was known about his family. He had a girlfriend, but she separated from him before the sentence.

Anirudh was a little concerned upon learning about the donor's past. He told Takashi, 'I expected a donor with a neat and decent history. On the contrary, what I found is very disturbing with a criminal past. Don't you think it will have an effect on the way the machine performs?'

'We have tried our best to find a better donor. Lack of time and availability of options might have led the management to get this donor. Anyways, we will have the override controls with us. Therefore, it should not be much of a concern,' replied Takashi. All metal parts are made of super alloy, a new alloy stronger than any metal in use till date. It is indeed made with seven different metals, including iron and titanium, which are considered to be strongest metals till date. There is of course a super memory chip and a central microprocessor made with the latest technology.'

'So all we have to do is to assemble,' said Maria.

'Nah, assembling can be done by anyone who follows certain instructions. This is a very complex thing as we need to assemble the mechanical parts and sync them with the human parts. That is going to take the skin out of us. Eventually, testing is also crucial. We have to pass the machine through various tests and go on testing till it is completely ready for use,' replied Anirudh. 'So, guys, this is it. We are now ready to start the real work. The technology team and medical team will start early tomorrow. The spiritual team has to wait till their turn as it involves only the loading of the software.'

Next morning, four people made history by performing the first-of-its-kind of operation on the robot with a human body and heart and a machine brain and limbs. Each part of the body was assembled with utmost caution as any wrong move could ruin the entire plan. It took seven hours to complete the operation. There was an observation period of twenty-four hours, and after which, the machine was loaded with all the software needed.

It had been forty-eight hours. All members of the crew were present at the laboratory. The humanoid machine was placed inside a shielded glass. It opened its eyes and was behaving normally. The body's vital signs were also reported to be normal. Suddenly the team was applauding and jumping as each started congratulating one another. Between a lot of joy and fun, the operation was termed *successful*. The loading of software started, and the machine would be operational by the next morning. 'Good work done by you and your crew,' said Takashi.

'Thank you, and I wish to talk to Jon.'

'Okay, Mr Anirudh, I will arrange a videoconference tomorrow' replied Takashi.

Next morning, there was a videoconference with Jon.

'Good morning, everyone. I congratulate each one of you for this outstanding work. I appreciate your sincerity and commitment. You have indeed completed the project way before the stipulated time. It may appear simple, but I am aware that it is not as simple as it looks. It must have really taken a toll on you. Our selection itself was based on merit, and your achievements in your personal fields are the reason you are here. Now that this project is completed, I am giving everyone an option to stay back and be a part of our successful journey. Think it over as this chance comes once in a lifetime and I know you are all intelligent people to accept this offer. Lastly, I need to inform you that your balance amount for this project has been wired already and we will revise a new structure for your next assignment. Thank you, all! Thank you, Great God.'

'What do you all have to say on Jon's offer, Those people who want to renew their contract must stay back as I need to discuss the pay perks and other issues,' said Takashi.

Ibrahim, Anirudh, and Sarah left the room. They were now millionaires with 25 million credited to their accounts. They have decided to go on a fifteen-day tour to Bali, Indonesia. Ibrahim had already planned to start a school and a rehab centre in Ethiopia. While on their way out, each one of the colleagues applauded.

Chapter 7

Kuta Beach, Bali Island, 5.57 p.m.

The sunset at Kuta Beach was dazzling with rays piercing out from the clouds. The cool breeze swept across all corners. One couple was walking across the ocean with waves touching their feet as they walked hand in hand, soul to soul. She wore a skirt with a cotton top, and he was dressed in khaki trousers and a cotton shirt. The scene was the most picturesque and artistic view for painters and poets.

'The waves like time seem to be eternal, the only assured thing in this world,' said Sarah.

'I would like to add *love* to that list,' said Anirudh.

She smiled at him and held his hand tightly. He was delighted.

'Why do people go after material things when the real essence of joy is in love? A loveless life is daunting and expurgated,' said Anirudh.

'Awesome, now I see a poet in a scientist. Shall I call it adaptation?' asked Sarah.

'You may call it acclimatization,' replied Anirudh.

'It's getting dark. I think we should be heading towards the hotel.'

He reluctantly agreed, and they started heading back to the hotel. There was a sudden noise, and people started running haywire. Suddenly the serene beach turned frightening. As Anirudh tried to enquire the reason for the people's reaction, he set himself and Sarah aside and watched over the ocean. He stood amazed, and he could not believe his eyes. Sarah was trying hard to know what was happening from him, but he was not responsive. In no time, the giant creature started coming towards them, and they both started to run along with the thousands of people. There was chaos all around, leading to a stampede. They ran and ran till they got into the nearest building.

'Anirudh, is that the same creature which we have seen in the island?' asked Sarah.

'Yes, that's the same creature with a greater size. It's unbelievable, and I don't have words to express my feeling. How could they just . . .' Anirudh was confused and could not speak properly.

'How many have you seen?' asked Sarah.

'Apparently, I have seen seven such creatures and maybe more,' replied Anirudh.

It was 9 p.m. and dark and silent all across the streets. There was not even a sound of murmur. Anirudh hinted at getting back to the hotel room, but Sarah objected to it. She wanted a confirmation that they were out of danger. He was adamant, and they slowly started their way towards the hotel, which was a couple of blocks away. They finally reach the hotel, holding their nerves. The scene there was even more devastating as the entire hotel was filled with pool of blood. Some people died, and some were wounded badly and crying for help. The police and ambulance started their work, and Anirudh and Sarah did what they could by helping the wounded once to reach the ambulance. Soon it was morning, and Sarah still could not get the incident off her mind. She still had visuals in her mind of people shouting for help.

The morning news channels reported the incident as the most devastating and most frightening in the history of human civilization. There were about two thousand people reported dead and thousands wounded. People and religious groups started saying that the End of the world seems imminent. The world going towards extinction sounded intimidating, but there was no clue to either counter or support the statement. The most interesting fact was that there were similar types of incidents in four different places across the globe.

'Shall we blame ourselves for not informing the public about the strange and primitive creatures?' said Sarah.

'Not at all, we never thought this devastating outcome would happen. Who would have imagined that those fish-crocodile-lookalike creatures would create such a horror and overthrow the pride of human beings which we have built over the years?' replied Anirudh.

'Where have those creatures gone? Did they go back to the ocean or head to where people are?' asked Sarah.

'The cops said that most of them headed back to the ocean, while there are some other people claiming that they headed into the forest,' replied Anirudh.

'I think we should head back to New York,' said Sarah.

'Oh, I have already made the arrangements, and we are immediately leaving for Los Angeles within an hour,' replied Anirudh.

Soon they reached the airport. They were queuing in the security check when all of a sudden people started watching the news on the television, which was showing something unbelievable. Soon people thronged to the only viewable television. The two managed to sneak into a small space amongst the crowd. It was really unbelievable; the video footage was showing one man scaring away the same creatures into the ocean in South Africa. The video footage, which was recorded from a cell phone, had gone viral. In no time, people started calling him Man with Divine Powers, and some called him the Saviour. The media channels and the government sought his help or advice to curtail the situation in the affected areas. Sarah was in seventh heaven and shouted in joy. Anirudh was seen cheering at the new saviour of the world. People asked them whether they knew the person in the video, and they left the scene without answering. They boarded the flight and headed to America. The couple then had to catch another flight to New York due to the non-availability of flight from Bali.

On their arrival, Sarah was busy with so many calls from who were concerned of her safety. They also discussed the divine power possessed by the man named GG, who just managed to scare the gigantic creatures into the ocean.

'So the man we gave a life is called GG. Great God as referred by Jon on his last speech. I have some kind of negative feeling. I sense something fishy in the entire episode,' said Anirudh.

'You are thinking too much. Why don't you rest for some time?' said Sarah.

'No, I am serious, Sarah. I feel there is some connection between that creature and the machine we have made.'

'Yes, nothing new! Creatures are predators, and GG is the saviour. That's what people feel,' replied Sarah.

'My concern is that we might not have been informed that these creatures' DNA was manipulated, and I suppose that these creatures were hypnotized by GG, directing them to the ocean. It was a pre-planned act by the society, I suppose,' said Anirudh.

'I suppose all you are saying are mere assumptions and doesn't have any Solid proof,' replied Sarah.

Anirudh decided not to raise the issue further until the right time. He was silent to her response.

It had been one month, and Anirudh had decided to head back to India as he had to complete his commitments to work on a new missile technology. Soon he joined services again and started working on a new technology. He was so much involved in work for the next one month and had no access to phone calls or the television. One day there was a call from Sarah.

'Hey, baby. How are you? You are not taking my calls. Is that how you show love, and is that true love?' said Sarah.

'Come on, Sarah, I was involved in work so much I barely go out of my office. Understand me. I love you,' replied Anirudh.

'Listen to me carefully. There has been a lot of development since last month. Now GG has occupied prime time in all channels across the globe. His presence is growing day by day, and people in so many countries have already started calling him Great God. The concerning factor is that the machine has more powers than what we have actually built. Now I doubt whether the real intention behind building the machine is the same as what was declared before. Or perhaps it has been changed due to the pressure set by the sponsoring companies. Last month, GG has saved London from a nuclear bomb threat and saved children from a school which caught fire. He has now become a hero and saviour. Though I have denied your allegations, now I really smell a rat. You have to come down to New York urgently,' said Sarah.

'Well, I don't see much problem in the entire episode even if they have projected more than what we have designed. Maybe that was to create confidence in people's minds. If they want to get near to the people, why should we try to poke our nose into it? I think we have to stay off from that and instead be involved in our respective works. After all, One World, One People is no easy task to take up.'

After realizing the silence from the other end, Anirudh asked, 'Are you listening? Hellooo.'

'Yes, I am listening to you, Anirudh,' said Sarah.

'What happened to your tone? Is everything all right? Helloo.'

There was no response, and the phone was hung up.

What happened to her? She seemed all right when I returned to india. Does she want me to stay there? Maybe she is missing me a lot. I was involved in work so much that I have forgotten about the outside world. She asked me to come to New York immediately with reason being GG, which was just a pretext! Maybe she wanted to see me desperately. How stupid I am to leave her alone. I need to see her immediately. She needs me. Anirudh took a flight to New York in no time.

Chapter 8

JFK International Airport, 7 a.m.

Air India arrived, and so did Anirudh. He took a taxi to Sarah's office, keeping in mind the New York traffic woes. He finally reached the hospital's R & D section to meet Sarah. There he was told that she had not been to the office since the last fifteen days. Anirudh was in a state of shock. He realized that something was seriously wrong. He immediately rushed to her home after making several attempts to connect to her mobile phone.

He was in the front of door, ringing the door bell. After a couple of minutes, he became impatient; he made up his mind to enter her home through the window by breaking the glass. Suddenly the door opened. It was Sarah. She was wearing a robe, and her eyes were tired. The black circles around her eyes appear as if she had not slept for a long time.

'Hey, Sarah! What's up? I will not ask how you are doing as it is evident that you are not well,' said Anirudh. As Anirudh took her into his arms, she started weeping and crying out loud. He gently kissed her lips. She suddenly transformed from a dull and bored person to the most active with his presence. He understood how much she loved him, and he made a mistake by leaving her alone.

In the afternoon, they had lunch outside and later went to Niagara Falls.

'This is an amazing place, isn't it?' said Sarah.

'Yes, this is the most remarkable tourist spot I have ever seen. It shows the strength and awesome power of nature,' replied Anirudh.

'Now tell me what happened. I know you were on antidepressants from the last fifteen days. I want to know what went wrong in your life,' asked Anirudh.

'The reason is in front of me. It is you who have made me fall in love, and you disappeared all of a sudden without any trace. You have intruded, captured, and created a path, and suddenly you disappeared. What made you ignore me?' questioned Sarah.

'I have never ignored you before and will never do in the future. My love for you is genuine, and I stand by what I say for eternity. But my way of love is free from any expectations from the opposite side. I firmly believe that love should not be a weakness. Rather, it has to be a symbol of strength. Most importantly, love should not lead you to sickness as it has a miraculous power to cure many diseases,' said Anirudh.

'I may principally agree with you on whatever you have said about love, but I have lost my mother when I was merely seven years old. My father orphaned me by moving away with another lady. I have become stronger and have fought against all odds to come to this level. All my life, my pursuit for love continued till you came to my life. I couldn't believe my eyes at first. Soon you have shown me a wonderful world from which I am reluctant to come out. Maybe I am expecting too much from you, but your presence is my only soothing act. I can't really count on more important things in life than your love,' said Sarah.

Anirudh smiled for a while and said, 'I am equally happy and sad for what you have told me. I'm happy after hearing your love for me. I'm sad as you say there is no other important goal in your life. As far as I know about you, you strive for your cancer research more than your life. I don't deny that life without love is unimaginable, but there are certain circumstances that arise in our lives where we have to choose either love or responsibility. A far as I am concerned, I believe that love sets us free from all bondages and doesn't push towards captivity. I am always there for you, Sarah. You may choose to come with me now, leaving your unfulfilled goal open, or work towards achieving your goal first and come to me for eternity.' He held her arms and looked into her eyes. 'The decision is yours, and I will always respect your decisions.'

Sarah stiffened. She looked into his eyes intensely, hugged him, and said, 'Thank you for opening my eyes. Thank you for redirecting me towards my goal of life. I am at your debt again. If there is anything I could ever do for you—'

'Oh, stop it! Sarah, don't make me a stranger by all your words. I will always be yours'

They stayed at the same place till dark and then decided to go to a restaurant. They have entered a Chinese restaurant. The decorations were all in red, curtains, lamps, and even seats were red.

'I have little difficulty coping with red. Shall we move to another restaurant?' asked Sarah.

'I have heard that the food is delicious here and ambience is great too. This is the most famous Chinese restaurant in New York,' replied Anirudh.

'Okay, we will stay if you insist,' said Sarah.

'Anyways, you are going to watch me and not the surroundings, right? What shall I order?' asked Anirudh.

'I will go for soft noodles as I am not hungry.'

'Yeah, two soft noodles, but before that, get us two hot and sour soup,' ordered Anirudh to the waiter.

'Hey, check out who is on TV, being interviewed,' said Sarah.

'Oh, seems like things are going very fast. He's On TV already. That's outstanding,' said Anirudh.

'You seem to be okay about all the events going around our very surroundings. They are eyeing a very big chunk, I am sure. They are making use of all their sticks to achieve their goals,' said Sarah.

'No, you have a very wrong opinion on this, Sarah. I am watching everything, and I am only waiting for right time to act. I need substantial leads to corner Jon for this. All the speeches given by Jon to mankind on world peace seem to be just a cover-up of the actual clandestine intentions,' said Jon.

'What might possibly be those clandestine intentions?' asked Sarah.

'All we need to do is wait and watch till the right time comes,' replied Anirudh.

Meanwhile, an interview with GG had just started. 'Hello, everyone. Good evening and very warm welcome to our viewers. Today we have a special guest of honour in our studio, and he is none other than GG. Hi, GG. Thank you for accepting our request to join our TV tonight.'

It's all my pleasure. TV is such an effective medium for me to get an opportunity to meet so many people in different locations said GG.

It is much publicized that your name, GG, stands for Great God. Is it true that you consider yourself as God? Asked Interviewer

No, by no means I consider myself as God. I rather call myself a Great Giver. Replied GG

Interviewer immediately asked arduous question 'So you don't believe in God? But who are you, and how did you possess such magical powers? What is that you are trying to communicate?'

This time GG paused for three seconds of time before replying to TV interviewer, 'It is immaterial to know about my whereabouts. But it is important to know what I can give to people. The three Ps that people are devoid of are *peace*, *pleasure*, and *prosperity*. The earlier management of God was not successful in maintaining peace and tranquillity in this world. As per earlier religions, God has created every person equally, and people have also been told that he sees everyone with love and compassion. Then what is the reason for all the sufferings that are happening? Why is there a gap between the haves and have nots? Why are there differences based on races, religions, and castes? Why is everyone not equally intelligent or equally beautiful? This leads to the feeling that God has a biased nature and punishes people who don't bow in front of him. Now, is that not narrow-mindedness? So our regime is paving the way for a new system where there will be no requirement of God. We assure you that we will provide peace, pleasure, and prosperity'.

While GG still seemed stable, the interviewer has grown inconsistent as he was not at upper hand in an interview. Now he decides to ask some direct questions to corner GG. He starts with another question with serious expression on his face, 'You want to do something for the people, but with what authority and what status?'

GG replies with smile 'I may not have any position, but still I can do many things for the people and no one can question me.' With little grin on his face.

Interviewer asks his next question 'It is clear that you want to consider yourself as an alternative god. That's unique. Is it a dawn of a new religion or a new god alone? How is that possible?'

'That is very much possible. The people in this world have done outstanding work by creating democracy and republic. The entire system runs on tenets, such as

'By the people, for the people, and to the people'. I am surprised to observe that not much R & D has been done in terms of selecting gods. People in this world are more fascinated about finding the existence of aliens, but no one has ever imagined that God is above each and every living or non-living thing in this universe. The quest for finding aliens can't be fulfilled without understanding god. As quoted earlier that human beings have sent one excellent precedent by invention of democracy. It has been proven fact that elected form of government functions much better compared to monarchy or dictatorship. There is ruling party, which forms government and opposition party which is always in a fray to nail and overthrow ruling party and come in to power. Likewise, if there is a god, who is ruling the world now, there is every possibility that there is opposition which is a fray to start its reign on this world. And I represent the opposition, who is responsible, kind and loving and only solace to the billions of people who want to better life and vexed up with existing regime of god and looking for change. I respect the people's views and vow to stand for them, so my dear people "Be cautious and know whether your prayers are reaching the correct ones or they are being put in a cold storage. I am a proponent of new regime to change the management of God."'Said GG

Turning towards camera, the interviewer said 'Before, the bone of contention was God, but now, there are all new doctrines and theories on the possibility of having so many gods and a change of management. It's interesting but still confusing for a vast number of people. Tell me elaborately your plans. But it's time for a small commercial break. Please don't go away as we will be back with more to follow.'

'What is your take on that, Anirudh?' asks Sarah.

'We still have to carefully observe their moves as they have not done anything substantial to nail them,' replied Anirudh, taking a deep breath.

'Well, the food has come finally! Emm, I am hungry now! Shall we order for any snacks, Sarah?'

'No thanks. I can't wait for one more hour. I usually avoid going to restaurant on weekends,' replied Sarah.

Meanwhile, the interview resumed.

The interviewer starts conversation 'Hello and welcome back. My last question to GG was on the elaborate explanation on his plans'.

GG starts saying ' My plans can only be accessed through the mobile application GG or by calling our Call centre number 12008769009. In a nutshell, we provide solutions to all your problems just by doing the simple task of signing up in our One World, One People society.

The interview went very well and Trp ratings of that particular channel have skyrocketed. Even the interviewer had got pat by his higher-ups. The interviewer smilingly said ' Time is up for our programme, and we will meet next week, same time. Goodnight, and do take care of yourselves.'

'What do you think are they up to? Are they really ought to do something awry?' asked Sarah.

'Now we have to closely observe their movements. The day is not so far now when they expose themselves completely,' said Anirudh.

'Why can't we try to contact Jon on this and know from him directly?' said Sarah.

'I think it is too early to respond. We will rather wait for some more days till we are equipped with adequate testimonials to nail him,' replied Anirudh.

'I have an idea. Why can't we consult them through their mobile application and try to understand their plan?' said Sarah.

'That's better,' replied Anirudh, and soon he downloaded the application and tried contacting them. The application asked for payment details as the registration needed USD 300 for one-time non-refundable fee. They were astonished after seeing the mobile application as they had developed this particular application for the entire world with over 120 locations. They were apparently targeting the entire world and arranging meetings in 120 different locations around the world. The reason for choosing the application was probably due to security issues as the mobile application was encrypted and didn't need voice conversation or email exchange. They had finally registered and booked a slot for the gathering scheduled the next day in New York.

Chapter 9

Next morning, they were at the Park Inn hotel in New York, in an auditorium with a capacity of 1,000 people. The auditorium was jam-packed and reminiscent of a concert by a very popular band. The people were holding portraits of GG. Music was being played, and slogans lauding GG were heard.

'The GG fever has swept swiftly than I imagined,' said Sarah.

'Oh yeah, seems like GG is going to be a famous diva in no time. Let us see what exactly they are targeting,' replied Anirudh.

The microphones being tested had confirmed that GG would be on stage within a couple of minutes. The crowd started roaring much more and continued till GG appeared on stage and took at least ten minutes to calm them down.

GG now started saying, 'Helloooooooooooooooooo! How are you?'

The people responded with 'Great'.

'Seems like you have not taken your breakfast this morning, or have I gone deaf? Can you repeat?' asked GG.

People shouted with all their might 'Great!'

'Okay, now I got you, guys. You all know that it is customary to invite new people to our society. One round of applause for our new joiners. While I rejoice at the rejuvenating, scintillating existing members, I also welcome the new members. There are different ways for the members to reach here. Firstly, through our existing members with their nominating power called the Token of Love. Secondly, through worldwide lottery system called the Will of God. And finally, through our mobile applications and our 24/7 call centres called the Destined. Well, whatever the mode of entry might be, the members are treated equally, and they are given all the options to succeed in life. So what is important in life, or what is that you value the most and intend to do? It could be your desires, ambitions, and goals in life. I want an answer from our new members of the organizations. Yes, please do not panic as each one of you will get a chance to speak. Yes, your name and profession, please.'

'I am Tom from the West Coast. I work as a construction labourer and earn a petty amount. I too have dreams in life, and my dream is to travel in my own BMW car and date a renowned Hollywood actress.'

'And what more do you want?' asked GG.

'That is all, sir,' he replied.

'Yes, you, lady. You may speak.'

'Thank you for the opportunity to speak. I am married for ten years and without children. I want children of my own. The doctors have informed me about my medical condition, and it seems impossible for me to have children in this life. Can you help me?'

'Who is next? There, the person in blue shirt.'

'Sir, my dream is to become the CEO of my company and marry the daughter of the present CEO.' Everyone laughed.

'Yes, what's wrong in dreaming to grow big, and what's wrong in marrying a girl whom he loves, irrespective of her status? Nothing's wrong with that child,' said GG. 'To everyone who is present here in this auditorium, I will see you through your ambitions and desires without getting anything. Don't worry, I won't take back any of your desires that I will grant. But it is a rule of nature that you have to sacrifice something to gain what you aspire. Any clarification, please ask me,' said GG. 'Well, each one of you is filled with desires and ambitions, but surprisingly, no one asked about the God and the afterlife. I say that you will be bestowed with God's mercy, happiness will prevail upon you in this life, and the afterlife has been secured. How do you feel about these offerings? Great, isn't it?'

'Yes, that sounds great,' replied someone from the crowd.

'Yes, what about the rest of you all?' asked GG.

'Great!' was the loud and unanimous answer from the crowd.

'That's fantastic. I would like to know how many people really want to meet and have God. In this very group, I have come across so many people who have unfulfilled desires in their wish list, but did you all imagine what God likes to say about your ambitions? Well, I welcome your ambitions in your life, but what does the Big Boss or the Super Boss of the existing regime like to say? When I call someone the Big Boss or the Super Boss, it is God without any hesitation. The gods which you believe, irrespective of any religion, will call this a *sin*. Now I question this. It is outrageous to call it a sin to fulfil your desires. Your very desires have been implanted by God. Desires, jealousy, and greed are creations of God, and he expects humans to subside and lead a very ordinary life. This world is full of desires and fulfilment, thus we face the aftermath. That's going to be horrifying. Imagine the aftermath you will face by overthrowing someone and sitting on his chair and marrying his daughter or wife. The crux of the situation lies there. Now what would be the immediate reaction? Retaliation. Now, what's the fun in doing or aspiring things which may lead you to the most horrifying nightmares of your life? Often you see yourselves encircled by your wants and desires at the same time your inability to reach your destination. Now tell me, how many of you have thought of committing suicide? Or how many of you think that about 90 per cent of your desires in life were reduced to compromises due to various circumstances arising out of life?

'Okay! Now that's an uncountable number of people who think that their lives are taking them nowhere towards fulfilling their desires, and there is a substantial number of people who felt like committing suicide at least once. Now have you ever imagined who is controlling your life? Come on, I am least expecting an answer that God is controlling everything in your lives. Even if you think that God is supreme and he controls everything in your life, it doesn't hold well with the kind of description given in the holy texts of many religions. I have read almost all religions books, and I know that God, as per contemporary religions, is kind, loving, and selfless. I want each one of you present here to think why there is a lot of suffering prevailing in the world despite God's assurance that good will be safeguarded and bad will be punished. Why does unhappiness seem to have engulfed the entire world? And why does hopelessness seem to be omnipresent? Think! You will get the answers. Thinking costs you nothing, so think as much as you can, and you will find the solutions. I will rather make your life easy by giving you options. What if you lead a happy life with all your desires fulfilled and all ambitions met without compromising your morals and your safety. That's great, isn't it?'

'Yeahhh,' responded the people.

'So...I am GG, asking you to join our society to lead a successful life. Before that, I wish to show you the success stories of our members. My personal assistant, Santanam, will take you through the video presentation.'

'Hello, ladies and gentlemen, and I welcome you aboard. Please have a look at our members sharing their success stories.'

Meanwhile, Anirudh and Sarah were jolted to see Santanam and quite surprised to see him as the personal assistant to GG. They tried to reach him, but the security personnel stopped them. They decided to stay till the presentation was over and then tried to approach Santanam.

As the video presentation went on, it showed people enjoying their lives and still believing in God. The beautiful presentation with catchy visuals left one question: 'How are people satisfied and yet believe in God and, more importantly, without compromise?' Of course, this question had to be answered by none another than the Great God, GG.

'Welcome back to the real world. Hope you have enjoyed the video presentation. That is just a sample collection. The actual lives of members are fantastic, fun-filled, and flamboyant. No words whatsoever to explain. I understand that one thing bothers you—being satisfied and being a devotee of God. Now how is that possible? I would like to hear some clues from you all.' Said GG

'I think we have to forgo some of our desires and pray and give thanks to God for what he has given.' Said anirudh silently from crowd.

'There is no question of foregoing anything! I will be responsible for your happy living. I take a divergent view on most existing religious theme on "Hail god and laud him for what he has given", I would rather ask people to pray god for only fulfilling dreams and not for all generic things he has given. That is a major tenet followed by our regime,' replied GG.

'Maybe we have to dream and only aspire for things within our purview.' Said sarah from crowd.

'There are no limitations to our aspirations and no rules to be followed in aspiring. There is no question of subsiding,' replied GG. 'Any further questions?'

Silence crept across the entire auditorium.

'I will break the ice,' GG started. 'The contemporary religions have been unanswerable to many things bothering the common man. Quite more than answering, you all doubt whether someone is really out there who listens to you and takes care of your well-being. There is no direct or indirect contact with God. Are your prayers been wasted? Is your belief in God blind? When we are not governed properly, why should we still believe in the tenets prescribed in the religious texts? So if there is God, why is he not visible? Are all your beliefs mere manifestations? Who is God to normal people, and what is prayer? Yes, it is me who is going to answer all your questions and free your mind to choose a correct path.

'First and foremost, the existence of God has been a subject of debates for more than 500 years. This perhaps is answerable by none other than God himself. Time and again, God has failed in responding to these questions. If God is unable to understand and fulfil the basic requirements, then what is the purpose of his existence?

'Your prayers to God have gone unnoticed as time and again he has shown that 90 per cent of your desires are unfulfilled. He creates a platform and also creates liveliness filled with unending desires. At the same time, he creates a barrier for everything to create fight between fellow human beings. I think they just follow because they are frightened. Do you all still believe in God, or are you intimidated by him? What if there is no God and only a friend or person next door substituting him? Think and think seriously. It would be amazing if there is a person or thing to substitute God whom we would have a direct access and we can post your dreams in life on the mobile application and our dreams will be fulfilled. There will be no rules and no one to regulate your wishes and challenge your decisions. It is you who decide for your life and not the so-called destiny.

'Destiny. The protracted debate on destiny still goes to the pinnacle. People who believe in destiny are people who give up and live pathetic lives where the body, mind, and soul don't coincide. Destiny had in fact held back our world by at least 100 years. Our society, One World, One People, considers destiny repudiation. Our society believes in go-getters and achievers.

'So we have reached the point where our minds, bodies, and souls have been pressing for change—the change in what we do, the change in what we follow, and the change in the way we pray. All these can be achieved by our simple process of membership. There are three kinds memberships based on your preferences. Our relationship managers are here to help you to register yourselves and your dear ones for the journey of life. With just a simple registration, you start your journeys. Now I would like to ask people who are interested in taking membership to stay back, and others may have refreshments and high tea in the dining area. Thank you for coming,' GG completed the session.

Anirudh and Sarah decided to stay back. They were looking for a chance to meet Santanam to enquire on the actual intention. They realized that one person was making all kinds of signs, inviting them to the lobby. He was exactly Santanam.

'Why are you people here, and why are you trying to put my life in danger?' asked Santanam, who looked frightened.

'What's going on, Santa? We want to know everything about this thing. And why is your life in danger? I, in fact, smell that everything is fishy. I need complete details,' asked Anirudh.

'What will you do? These people are very powerful— politicians, businessmen, and religious heads who dominate our daily world. I beg you to leave this premise if you want to see me alive,' said Santanam.

'Okay, we are leaving now, and I will be waiting for you by 11 a.m. at Café Classic Inn, Times Square,' said Anirudh.

Soon Anirudh and Sarah left the hotel and reached Sarah's home.

As Sarah looked at Anirudh seriously, he said, 'Are you afraid of our lives being taken?'

'No, not now, I am afraid of Santanam's life being in danger as it is very likely that their society's people have seen us talking to him. I think he might not turn up to meet us as planned.'

'Shall we try meeting him now, Sarah?' replied Anirudh.

'Let's try calling him.'

Anirudh made a call, but Santanam's mobile seemed to be switched off. He remembered Santanam giving another personal number which he shared only to selected people. He dialled it, and the mobile number was connected and ringing.

Chapter 10

'Hello, Santanam.'

'Are you crazy? I told not to follow me. Do you want me dead?'

'I just wanted to know the entire thing,' replied Anirudh.

'Why do you want to know? You will not be able to change anything. These people, as I already told you, are very powerful people, and you are simply inviting trouble for you and Sarah,' said Santanam.

'I only want answers to a few questions,' replied Anirudh.

'What questions? Ask me in two minutes as I can't talk to you more than two minutes from the bathroom,' replied Santanam.

'What is that membership, and who is the new god they were talking about?' asked Anirudh.

Santanam: Membership is the signing up and getting into the One World, One People society. Once they are part of that society, they will get everything they want—employment, a luxury car, desired women, and so on. In turn, they have to use only products manufactured by syndicate companies with the hologram GG and stay only in buildings built by the builders of the syndicate. The society initially fulfils every dream of the members, including his desired position in the office at work or a date with the most famous Hollywood actress. Subsequently, the society uses a person's position and power to get new members to sign up. The members are made to go through meditation classes, where they are sedated and dreams are implanted in their brains, and then they are brought into consciousness. This is the method they employ to fulfil his new dreams with the available resources. This activity goes on, but when they find that the person is no longer useful, he will be made to believe that his body no longer sync with his desires and will be sent to the reincarnation stage, where his complete memories are recorded and implanted into another person to be released in public as a reincarnated member to gain trust amongst people.

Anirudh: How are dreams fulfilled, especially desires to date the most famous Hollywood pop stars?

Santanam: One World, One People is a vast society with people from all walks of life and all kinds of professions. So they face no difficulty in convincing a member to go on a date with another member. There is no barrier as they follow no rules and no commitment, just fulfilment of desires. Hence, nothing is called sinful or wrong. Here, anyone can sleep with anyone without any hassle. Just in case a desired celebrity or person is not a member, A clone is made and sent to that person. Our ex-colleague Dr Maria heads the team of making clones.

Anirudh: Is it only about sexual fulfilment, or is there more to it?

Santanam: Oh! There is more to it, my friend. Sex is just a driving force. Some may desire a better position at the workplace, which can be fulfilled if it falls under a member company. In other cases, the position is given to a person with the help of their strong and worldwide network. Members' fulfilment of desires is only the tip of the iceberg. Earlier, there were only twenty member companies, but it extended to about two hundred strong member companies and it seems like nothing is impossible to them. In turn, they are boosting their product sales in a faster way with much inflated rates. Their net sales seem to grow 1,000 per cent. They also run eleven governments of mostly African and Asian nations and had affiliations to other powerful countries and leading banks, corporate hospitals, medical insurance companies, and so on.

Anirudh: Now how is that related to religion?

Santanam: Religion is the core sector for them as they see religion as detrimental in achieving their objective, and also, they see religion as a lucrative business too. Most people who are stubborn as mules become complacent on religious reverence. Hence, they see religion as a big business worldwide and an obstacle to achieve their goals. There are no rules and regulations amongst members of the society. No marriages, only partnerships. Only members shall be treated at their designated hospitals with cure to most of the diseases. Members are used as organ donors on the pretext of reincarnation. They believe in GG as the ultimate super god. There is no messenger or prophet, and there is direct access to this god. They follow religion in a new way. They use the mobile application for sending their problems and desires and videoconferencing for meditation. Also, they attend society-sponsored meetings to share their success stories. They indeed call the entire thing a religion as the basic tenets is self-fulfilment.

Anirudh: What are their motives and goals?

Santanam: They are aiming something very big as they view the world as a vast market. They want to create two different worlds—the world of the members and the world of the non-members. With major companies and powerful banks on their side, the other non-member nations would face marginalisation. The only solace offered was to join as member countries. I need to go now as any kind of doubt may cost my life. Need to tell you that Jason got killed!

Anirudh: Jason got killed? But how?

Santanam: Jason got involved so much in their business, that he knows too much to be alive, We don't have time to discuss that now. Listen to me carefully. They have got every information about you all, and they will reach you in no time.

Anirudh: Now tell me how to reach the island we have worked earlier.

Santanam: I have to hang up my phone now. Even I am not aware of that. But I know the latitude and longitude. Write it down.

Santanam's phone hung up before telling anirudh the coordinates of the island.

'What next?' questioned Sarah.

'We have to urgently call Ibrahim for help and also gather Maria and Santanam to discuss the way forward. I think the information we got through mobile is not complete, and there must be plenty more things to know, but the information we have is enough to put fear in us,' replied Anirudh.

'Maybe we need to call Ibrahim first,' said Sarah.

'No, our voices have been sampled. They will recognize us from anywhere we call irrespective of the mobile number we dial. I think we need to go directly to Ethiopia,' replied Anirudh.

Next evening, they reached Bole International Airport. Soon they took a bus to reach Ibrahim's village, located about 100 kilometres away from Addis Ababa City. It was a small village with metal roads, good sanitation, and greenery at every corner. There appeared a school called Fatima School. The couple entered to see students interacting with Ibrahim.

They decided not to disturb them and waited for the lecture to finish. After concluding the session, Ibrahim responded happily upon seeing them.

'Great that you have come to see me and my work. I am very glad to see you people. You must be tired, so let's go my home and have some food and then talk about my project and the challenges I have to face in completing the school and one hospital. Apart from that, we will visit the entire village. The Ethiopian government had now declared this village as a model village. I will show you how I developed it and what exactly the social development is,' said Ibrahim.

Anirudh and Sarah were stiffened by the response they received and didn't want to spoil his happiness. They decided to go to ibrahim's home and meet his family and then discuss further topics.

They reached home; it was a small house, but well organized and decorated. They found it in contrast to the expectation they created in their minds after seeing a big school and hospital in a very big sprawling campus.

Ibrahim soon caught their weird responses and said, 'You must find at my home very small against all your expectations. Yes, I spent little for my home as we barely live here. My wife looks after the administration of the hospital. My children are in the school hostel—yes, the same school which I have built for the orphans who lost their families in wars and terrorist attacks. Now I can make out from you that you have come to me for a different purpose. We'll talk about that, but first, you have to take a shower and have some food.'

Ibrahim introduced his wife, Kathija. She cooked a traditional Ethiopian food *wat*.

'My wife cooks all Ethiopian and African dishes. How does it tastes?' asked Ibrahim.

'It is very tasty. But, little bit spicy,' replied Sarah.

'Not at all. I am from India, the land of spices, and I find this special dish tasty and can be delicious with some more spices,' replied Anirudh.

They enjoyed their meal and interacted on various issues for more than one hour. Later Ibrahim asked the reason for their visit.

'Ibrahim, we have been misled by Jon of One World, One People society. They have grown manifold in the past months. The society is run by topmost industrialists and politicians to reach their objective within a short span. Religion and people's beliefs are being used as a mascot for their clandestine inner ambitions. We are socially responsible and directly related to this particular project, so we have to stop this before it's too late,' said Anirudh.

'I've expected that this will happen one day, but since I needed the money to fulfil my ambition to start a school for the orphaned children, I signed up for the project. But what can we do in this regard? I think it's already too late now. We are minnows now and too weak to take down these powerful people who have presence everywhere.'

'But we have created GG, and we have the technique to override and turn him towards us,' said Sarah.

'Whatsoever, I am extremely sorry that I will not be able to join you in your quest to know and stop all this. I am now restricted to run the school and hospital for the betterment of the people here,' replied Ibrahim.

Anirudh silently responded, 'It is shocking yet understandable. I will not force you. You have been chasing your ambition to do something for the future generations. Your establishment of a school and hospital is only a step towards the fulfilment of your goal. Now you have more responsibilities than ever. But my only concern is that they are planning to divide the world into two to have their clutches on the economies of world. Every citizen of the world is either directly or indirectly affected by this. Jason already lost his life, and Santanam's life is in grave danger.'

'What is happening? I have never imagined that they could take away people's lives. I only have a doubt in my mind that the project will be, at some point in time, controlled and steered by capitalistic people. But they seem to be out of bounds now. They are targeting people. In some way, we too are responsible for this fiasco, and I don't want anyone in the future generation to hold me responsible for this. Now that we have created a monster, we must have the power internally to curb and keep it under wraps. Tell me if you have anything in your minds, or shall I plan the coup?' asked Ibrahim.

'Now that's like the Ibrahim I know,' said Anirudh with a smile.

'Finding the place is not at all difficult. Remember, we were airlifted from Miami to the island, and the time taken was about two hours. So probably, we must have been taken to a secluded, uninhabited island between the two American continents as there are fewer chances of presence of any island towards east. When we stayed in the island, I kept an eye on the supplies which arrived through small boats, so there is a chance that the supplies were being transported from the nearest dock area. I also noticed that the products we used were primarily made in the USA, but the milk, fruits, and vegetables were supplied from a nearby farmland. I noticed *chaconia* flowers were commonly found in the island, which happens to be the national flower of Trinidad and Tobago, and dairy products of the brand Anchor, which also coincidentally belongs to the same country,' said Anirudh.

'You are such a geek,' complimented Sarah.

'Okay, we shall now leave for T and T and try to find a clue by observing the dock areas from where our supplies were taken to the island,' said Ibrahim.

Now the three of them left for T and T and then chased one transport boat from a speedboat. They finally entered the island. They were trekking into the island but still there was no clue whether they were in the correct destination. After forty-five minutes of walking, they finally saw the centre.

Chapter 11

Anirudh looked triumphant and started saying, 'So finally we have reached. We have made our first step successfully, and more steps to follow.'

As he looked behind, his shoulders shrugged, and his eyes were reluctant to believe that Sarah and Ibrahim were taken into custody by a few armed men. Before he tried to say something, he was beaten at the back of his head. The three of them were taken to a secluded place, and confined.

Sarah opened her eyes and realized they were held captive and placed in a small cabin by the lake. She tried to wake the other two, but she was unable to cope with her low energy levels. finally, with great difficulty, she managed to wake them up. They seemed to be out of thoughts and waiting for any sort of help.

'Don't be foolish, you fellows. No one will turn up here,' said Sarah.

'We just can't wait till we get killed. *Need to hit something till we are alive,*' replied Ibrahim.

'Don't worry, guys, I have an idea. Remember we were given one encrypted coding which was not in the plan? I will tell you, don't you strain your brains. We have created one signal system which resets the total function of the machine we have created, and all its existing commands will be deleted, resetting the machine to the same stage when we have introduced it to Jon.'

'Yes, that's unbelievable, but can we rely on that?' asked Ibrahim.

'Why not? If you people have trust in me, then just follow the instructions. I know it is very hard to follow, fierce meditation for 7 minutes will create wave signals and reach GG. But we have no other cards to play,' said Anirudh.

'You call yourself an atheist? Then how come you believe in meditation?' questioned Sarah.

'Meditation has nothing to do with my being a believer or non-believer. Rather, it is a science through which we can send signals by generating waves from our brains as you are aware that the human body can generate electricity by itself. A few animals have the capability to read heat signatures, and snakes have scales which can read enemies through waves. Likewise, the human brain can serve as a telecommunication tower to send codes or signals,' replied Anirudh. 'I have no time to explain all this, just follow what I say. We need to hold our hands together and meditate for seven minutes. I will make things clearer. We have to hold hands and concentrate on nothing—that is, think of nothing for seven minutes. Remember, any one person getting distracted will put the entire thing into the same position, so be careful.'

'Are you talking about telepathy? Asks sarah.

'A form of telepath, but more advanced than telepath. It was kind of an art widely practiced in ancient India called

"Dhyan Sampark", which is still in practice in very few areas in india. Yes, that is very much possible,' replied Anirudh.

'We've been trying for one and a half hours. But we are not able to connect to GG. I think now it is an impossible task,' said Ibrahim.

There was a noise from someone going inside the cabin, and they realized that it was Jonathan Reynolds.

'Hi, guys! Hope you are doing better now,' said Jon sarcastically.

'Is this the way you treat your friends?' asked Ibrahim furiously.

'*Friend* is a word which has so many definitions. Well, most importantly, "A friend in need is a friend indeed" is a widely publicized proverb. I have a special definition for *friend*: "There are no permanent friends or enemies in politics." Well, I have mastered in political science and dreamed of leading the world by establishing the largest and most vibrant political regime. Here I am, expected to lead the world in a couple of years. I am able to achieve this feat with minimum bloodshed. Where the likes of Alexander the Great and Genghis Khan have failed to achieve, I am able to do successfully. After all, I believe in discussions, negotiations, and takeovers, and not wars, violence, and conquest. Don't you call me intelligent?'

'You are foolish to even imagine. People and media have been watching your moves carefully. In no time, your entire system shall be reduced to zero, and you will end up in prison for the rest of your life,' replied Anirudh with perhaps clenched teeth.

'Which media are you talking about? Those which received kickbacks for the exclusive coverage that made GG a superhero overnight by scaring away a few creatures? In fact, those creatures were products of our laboratory. Don't even try to speak on behalf of the people. They are selfish and coward. They want to lead healthy and luxurious lives with nothing to do with morals and God. It is unlikely that people or the media will come to your rescue,' said Jon.

'We are not bothered about our lives. We are much bothered about the innocent people who are being pushed under your regime,' said Ibrahim.

'You seem to be very emotional about people. All your life, you have wasted your time reading religion texts. You must read people's minds, which I did successfully. People expect peace, luxury, and safety, and they don't need a god. They keep on praying to a god who never responds to their questions and never comes to their rescue when they are in need. Your form of god is selfish and expects people to be afraid of him. It's the very point we have been capitalizing. We are now providing a god who can interact and help his people and who can offer luxury of women, home, good lifestyle, free medical treatment, and safety for all. You need not worry about terrorist threats. As there are no religions, there are no terrorists or fundamentalists. We offer all this by doing a little work for us and using the products of our member companies. No one is bothered to search for the real god,' said Jon.

'Who told you that all people are alike? There are people who are very stubborn and look for reality and care about the morals even more than their lives. For those people, you are a devil whose words are like Evil's verses,' replied Ibrahim.

'Don't ever use those words as they stand no chance of survival nowadays. People are sensible enough as they have understood that your god enjoys violence and seeing human beings killing one another. He enjoys watching people being burned alive. He enjoys seeing women being gang-raped, and so on. He created this world and created people, and he created the atmosphere where people fight one another and kill one another. Okay, let's not talk about the existing god now. I am giving you a golden opportunity to join us and lead our society. I will ensure that happiness prevails in you all,' said Jon.

'There is no question of working under such a wicked person like you and for an unethical society with a band of thieves,' replied Sarah.

'Okay then, you shall die in pain. Guards, set them afire.'

Jon left as the guards locked the cabin and set it ablaze. In no time, fire engulfed the little cabin.'

Anirudh said, 'Let's presume that we are already dead and have no hard feelings of our failing in life as we don't exist. How do you feel? Are you feeling lighter than cotton?'

'Yes!' replied both.

'Then now let's hold our hands and try to connect ourselves, We need to send signals to reset the system with in GG, which will bring him back to normal. But, this connecting our energy souls need intense concentration to reach a point, which will send required signals to bring him back to normal, the saint we have initially created will be invoked' said Anirudh.

The three of them held their hands together as one unit and meditated fearlessly even under fire. It was after six minutes that the roof started collapsing on them. They could now feel the heat, but still, that did not stop them from focusing. They finally found themselves in perplexity, leading towards a bright light resembling incandescent sunlight with more luminosity than sunlight.

Chapter 12

Anirudh tried hard to understand what was happening until he found himself alone in front of the bright light. He felt lighter as if he were floating, blissful and free from all bondages of the world. He wanted to say something but could not utter anything as he felt completely filled with knowledge and there was nothing else to question. Never had he felt happier than that moment, and never had he imagined that he would experience complete fearlessness, euphoria, and perdurability. It was unbelievable how a person who once questioned everything found himself satisfied without any questions. It was as though all knowledge had been transmitted into his brain.

Suddenly he was disturbed by someone. They were taken out with woollen blankets covering their bodies. The people who were carrying them were the armed guards, and the instructions were passed on from GG. When Anirudh realized that he was still alive, he began to visualize the surroundings, and GG stood in front of him.

'I hope you are feeling better now, Mr Anirudh and Ms Sarah. I have given the information on clandestine intentions of this society to all the governments and press. All the people involved were arrested, and UN has called for enquiry and deployed one task force to see to it that such things will never happen in the future.'

'Where is Ibrahim?' asked Anirudh.

'He passed away due to haemorrhage,' replied GG.

'RIP Ibrahim,' said Sarah.

'Maybe he was so touched by divinity that his soul was reluctant to come back,' said Anirudh.

'I am unable to comprehend what you want to communicate,' said Sarah.

Anirudh smiled at Sarah and asked, 'Did you experience anything after we have meditated?'

'Yes, I did experience some bright light, and I realized that I was being saved by a few people sent by GG. I was happy that we were successful and have managed to reset the system of GG, bringing him back to his normal position. The Signals we have sent have reached GG eventually. At the same time, I was concerned as you and Ibrahim were still unconscious and not breathing. After numerous efforts of the doctors, you managed to get consciousness.'

'Now I realize that among the three of us Ibrahim was the most spiritual person and next to him was me, an atheist. Yes, an atheist is a person who questions the existence of God, and in that process, he makes himself most sought after by God. God always wanted to reach the people who question his very existence rather than the people who believe in blind worship.'

'You mean to say that you have seen God?' asked Sarah.

'No one sees God, we only experience him. And this can be possible at any time, anywhere, and for everyone if the thought is genuine.'

'Now I see change in you drastically! Suddenly you have become Guru Anirudh,' said Sarah.

'Not exactly, I have not changed at all, but my direction and pace of journey in this world have changed. It is like reaching a lake after a long walk in a desert, and it is like searching for a destination for your entire life and finally finding that the destination is nothing but your inner self.'

'Oh, you are taking me to heights of confusion. I think you need a break! Shall we plan for another holiday trip?' asked Sarah.

'Now I have realized that every day is Sunday and every day can be a holiday. The only difference is that there are no specified activities for these holidays or, for that matter, no specified work to be done in working days,' said Anirudh.

Sarah stared at him and looked astonished on his spiritual talk. She said to him, 'I think we have to see a doctor immediately.'

Anirudh smiled and decided not to talk about anything on any subject further as it was taking her into chaos. He simply said, 'We now have great responsibilities on our shoulders as we need to complete Ibrahim's dream and at the same complete ours.'

'Okay, now that's a characteristic of Mr Anirudh, a taskmaster.'

Soon the representatives of various channels thronged Anirudh and Sarah, asking multiple questions.

'My only answer to all of you that, time and again, it has been proved wrong to think on religious lines to unite society. Religion, sect, colour, and creed have failed to deliver a sense of belongingness. We have to focus on diversity that prevails all around. When nature explains the rule of coexistence, how can we defy and create rift amongst people of the same species? Hence, we are made to coexist and live in harmony.'

Anirudh now ran a chain of schools for the underprivileged in India and Africa, with Ibrahim's widow heading the organization with name *the Path*.

Sarah spent more time in her research and would occasionally go to South America to conduct free health camps. Both Anirudh and Sarah spent summers in their new home in Ladakh in north India.

'Oh, such a beautiful place on earth. I want to spend the rest of my life on this part of the world with your company,' said Sarah.

'The real beauty is in the way you look at things. There are so many beautiful moments that can be felt or experienced without any visuals. We are born to pass that message to people,' replied Anirudh.

'Does it means you have plans to publish a book or something?' asked Sarah.

'We have made something which has more information than books and is more sophisticated than smartphones. The traits we have embedded make it unique and stand as a selfless, fearless, and effective leader. Yes, I am talking about none other than GG. What else can we employ to propagate our motto?'

The quest for God continues as the real essence of feeling God is not on searching for supernatural power but on experiencing the divinity within you and others. All you have to do is enlighten.

Printed in the United States
By Bookmasters